THE HOUSE OF ULYSSES

THE HOUSE
OF ULYSSES

A NOVEL BY JULIÁN RÍOS

Translated by Nick Caistor

Dalkey Archive Press
Champaign and London

Originally published in Spanish as *Casa Ulises* by Editorial Seix Barral, S. A., 2003
Copyright © 1991, 2003 by Julián Ríos
Translation copyright © 2010 by Nick Caistor
First edition, 2010

Library of Congress Cataloging-in-Publication Data

Ríos, Julián.
  [Casa Ulises. English]
  The House of Ulysses / Julián Ríos ; translated by Nick Caistor. -- 1st ed.
    p. cm.
  Originally published in Spanish as Casa Ulises in 2003.
  ISBN 978-1-56478-597-8 (pbk. : alk. paper)
  1. Joyce, James (1882-1941)--Appreciation--Fiction. 2. Joyce, James, 1882-1941. Ulysses-
-Fiction. I. Caistor, Nick. II. Title.
  PQ6668.I576C3713 2010
  863'.64--dc22
                    2010025818

Partially funded by the University of Illinois at Urbana-Champaign and by a grant from the
Illinois Arts Council, a state agency

This publication was partly supported by a grant from the program for Cultural Cooperation
between Spain's Ministry of Culture and United States Universities

This work has been published with a subsidy from the Directorate-General of Books,
Archives and Libraries of the Spanish Ministry of Culture

www.dalkeyarchive.com

Cover: design and composition by Danielle Dutton
Printed on permanent/durable acid-free paper and bound in the United States of America

THE HOUSE OF ULYSSES

THE ULYSSES MUSEUM

ANTECHAMBERS

STEP INSIDE

Step inside and take a look, or perhaps he said a book, sweeping his magic wand in a semicircle in front of him. Our Cicerone in rigorous black with a purple polka-dot bow tie, long-legged and pallid, white streaks in chestnut hair smoothed back with brilliantine, a blind man's glasses, a straggly moustache. Like an ice-skater or Fredasteric* dancer he glided across the Museum's wide black-and-white checkerboard floor.

Almost at once among the groups of visitors the beanpole unanimously baptized as the "man with the Macintosh" (a Macintosh computer, that is) stood out, the machine he was frequently

---

* Or perhaps "fredasthenic."

to consult slung over his shoulder, although he never said a word. His exact opposite was also immediately visible, thanks to the great flabby rolls of his humanity and his affable demeanor. This fifty-year-old with a Yankee nasal drawl presented himself to left and right as Professor Ludwig Jones, Phi Beta Kappa, like some great bear or Orsonwellian Falstaff about to burst the seams of his lizard-green tweed suit.

A gaggle of lost Japanese ladies goggled at each other and cried triumphantly: Nora! then fired off their cameras, Mari-on! as they entered the labyrinth of screens and panels where photographs and captions offered a detailed chronology of *The Works and Days of James Joyce*.

THE ABC OF *ULYSSES*

Flanked by the rotund Professor Jones on my right, and the strange Macintosh man still staring at his computer screen on my left, we began to gather round the Cicerone. The circle was unbroken by three readers carrying (each one, one each) a volume of the monumental illustrated edition of *Ulysses* in three parts: a lanky gent with a white-flecked beard wearing prehistoric white overalls; to his left, the slender form of a dark-haired girl poured into in a pair of white shorts, cropped hair and laughing black eyes ("eyes full of night") over the indigo "*Ulysses* Museum" T-shirt, fronted and back-sided by Joyce; to her left, a few paces away, wrapped in a grayish coat with bulging pockets, the tiny old man with white locks and crackling breath, sucking on an extinguished pipe.

The mature reader (did she call him Ananias?), the young female reader (Babel or Belle?), and the old critic. Let's call them A, B, and C, for short.

At the back of the first antechamber, we were now contemplating the painting, *Joyce Contemplating the Bust of Homer*. This depicts the author of *Ulysses* lost in thought, left hand at his waist, and right hand resting on the marmoreal garlanded head of the author of the *Odyssey*.

Here's Homer, A exclaimed in Latin, and his disciple.

Both of them in blind-men's glasses, B said.

Homerici oculi, Professor Jones chimed in, also practicing his Latin. Eminent Homerians.

HAPPY IS HE, WHO, LIKE ULYSSES . . .

When Joyce was twelve, the Cicerone was telling us, he read Charles Lamb's *The Adventures of Ulysses*, and that same year had no hesitation in choosing Ulysses as the subject for an essay on "My Favorite Character," which he was asked to write for his English class at the Jesuit Belvedere College in Dublin.

A choice he chose forevermore, said A. There was no one like Ulysses.

For Joyce, Ulysses was a hero all too human, explained the Cicerone, with his weaknesses and virtues as husband, father, lover, and son, voyaging through a lifelong odyssey filled with shipwrecks and adventures. His proverbial caution and cunning allowed him to overcome all his trials. In the final reckoning, Ulysses was a good man, or at least that was what Joyce concluded, years after he had finished his own *Ulysses*.

He didn't condemn him as Dante did, by putting him in his *Inferno*, C observed. Yes, Ulysses (as Joyce also said of Bloom) was a good man. As well as the fascination the *Odyssey* had held for Joyce since childhood, becoming for him The Book, Homer's epic poem, containing as it does almost every kind of human experience, also served as a reference point to set limits for an undertaking that risked becoming infinite and, in the same way that he later used Vico's cycles of history to help him structure *Finnegans Wake*, it was very useful to him to bring order to chaos.

His comic magma, said A, or his *chaosmicomedy*. Joyce of course compressed the twenty-four books of the *Odyssey* into twenty-four hours of a day in Dublin.

C agreed, and pointed his pipe at the figure of Joyce in the center of the painting:

Obviously he had no wish simply to tell us Homer's mythical story all over again, or to present a parody of it, a farce. Instead, Joyce used it for very personal ends (so personal they are occasionally almost private) without always being bound by its structure. Throughout the eight years it took him to compose his magnum opus, he took from it what he felt he needed at every moment.

The basic outline, A said, was also a way of referring to a shared experience . . .

Especially in those days, C muttered, biting the stem of his pipe, when the study and reading of the classics was more in vogue.

Yes, said A, and it was also a way of referring to the secret unity of literature through ages and cultures. As if Joyce wanted to reveal his sources: my myth and me.

I think you can track his sources more closely, B objected, if you study a map of Dublin and the Thom's Directory for 1904.

No, don't let Professor Nabokov lead you astray, said Professor Jones. Homer's imperishable odyssey and the study by Victor Bérard on *The Phoenicians and the Odyssey* (Paris: 1902–1903) are the best Baedeker to use to follow the traces of the GreekJew or JewGreek Leopold Bloom.

In the end, the mythical is Semitical, said A.

The two are not mutually exclusive, C said. The map of the Mediterranean can be superimposed on the map of Dublin. Homer can exist alongside the streets of Dublin.

Mare Nostrum and *Mare Magnum*, said A. Joyce putting Mulligan's dream of Hellenizing Ireland into practice.

Greek fireworks . . . said B with a smile.

You have to discover the Mediterranean in Dublin Bay, A said. Curiously enough, *Ulysses* opens and closes with two Mediterranean decantings or displacements. Joyce's novel starts in the famous Martello tower, which in fact is a Mediterranean fortress, copied by the English, as its name suggests, from one at Punta Mortella in Corsica. So the tower was displaced from the Mediterranean to Dublin Bay. That tower is the *omphalos*—as Mulligan himself says—the navel of the classical and yet modern world of *Ulysses*. And Joyce's novel ends with a golden flourish (or at least a brass

one in the jingling bed Molly brought from Gibraltar to Ireland).
Another *non plus ultra*. It is there that Ulysses-Sinbad finally finds
rest. At the end of his voyage round the day in eighteen worlds.

Tired? asked B.

He rests. Takes a nap. He has traveled, A said.

I prefer to revisit the Dublin *Ulysses* rather than the *Odyssey*,
said B.

But our Cicerone did not hear her, or chose not to. He explained
that *Ulysses* had kept the triptych structure of the *Odyssey*: first the
"Telemachia," which as its name implies has Ulysses' son Telemachus for hero. After that, the *Odyssey* or "Ulyssedy" proper, covering the voyages and adventures of Odysseus or Ulysses, as he was
known in Latin. Then finally the "Nostos" or "Return," where the
hero regains his home after an absence of twenty years—ten in
the battle of Troy, another ten in his wanderings. At this point, the
Cicerone summarized the *Odyssey* in the not-always-orthodox
order of Joyce's *Ulysses*, announcing each part in a grave voice as
though they were stations—for travelers, or of the Cross . . .

PART ONE, OR TELEMACHIA

1. Telemachus

Young Telemachus is in Ithaca, dispossessed and powerless against
the suitors, led by Antinous and Eurimacus. They look down on
him arrogantly, destroy his home, and harass his mother Penelope, who is still faithfully waiting for Ulysses.

How old was Telemachus then? B wanted to know.

He was born shortly before the start of the Trojan War, said C. So he must have been around twenty.

2. Nestor

On the goddess Athena's advice, Telemachus assumes the guise of Mentor, Ulysses' faithful friend, and goes in search of his father. He reaches Pylos in the Peloponnese, where he seeks the advice of the wise old king Nestor, but Nestor has no news of where his father might be.

Nestor, said our mentor Professor Jones, was as talkative as he was wise. In our day, two species of parrot bear his name.

3. Proteus

Telemachus next visits the court of another of his father's comrades-at-arms: Menelaus, King of Sparta. Menelaus tells him the story of his eventful return from the Trojan War and his meeting with the "Old Man of the Sea," the sea-god Proteus, on the island of Pharos, close to the delta of the Nile. The slippery and ever-changing Proteus could not only adopt any form he pleased, but also had the gift of prophecy, which Menelaus could only wring from him when he managed to lay hands on him.

In front of Menelaus, said C, Proteus metamorphosed into a lion, a snake, a panther, a wild boar, water, and a tree.

But from Proteus, Menelaus learned that his comrade Ulysses was trapped by enchantment on a distant island, A said.

4. Calypso

On his return from Troy, Ulysses' ship was wrecked on the island of Ogygia, where he was held captive for seven years by the enchanting nymph Calypso. Then Athena interceded with Zeus, who sent Hermes to ask Calypso to allow Ulysses to go home. Reluctantly, the nymph agreed and offered Ulysses food and tools to help construct a raft.

Calypso's mysterious island is usually situated in the Straits of Gibraltar, said Professor Jones.

A sacrifice on the glib altar of love, A concluded.

"O, rocks!" said B raucously.

5. The Lotus-eaters

Ulysses is shipwrecked again, and arrives at the court of King Alcinous in Scheria, where he tells in great detail of all the vicissitudes and hardships he has suffered since he left Troy. At the start of their voyage, Ulysses and some of his companions had disembarked to find water in the land of the lotus-eaters who were very hospitable and friendly, and gave them the lotus to eat. This led them to lose their memory and all willpower. Ulysses' men became addicted to the fruit of oblivion and their chief had great difficulty in persuading them to return to their ships.

The lotus in the *Odyssey* is probably a shrub of the *Ziziphus lotus* species, said Professor Jones. It was used to make a fermented drink.

To drink is to forget, squawked A.

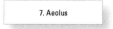

6. Hades

Ulysses descends to Hades, the kingdom of the dead, looking for the blind prophet Tiresias. He also meets the shades of several of his dead companions, such as Elpenor, and of his mother.

Poor Anticlea let herself die of sadness, said C. She could not bear her son's absence.

Without taking the parallel too far, said A, we should remember that the father of the Dublin Ulysses Leopold Bloom was also a suicide.

And it is likewise worth noting, said Professor Jones, that in Greek, "Hades," the god of the dead, means "The Invisible One." Appropriate, don't you think? he said, turning to the man with the Macintosh.

7. Aeolus

The god of the winds, Aeolus, tries to help Ulysses on his voyage of return. He gives him a leather bag containing all the adverse winds. Ulysses is dozing near the helm of his ship as it nears Ithaca, when some of his companions, thinking the bag contains treasure, open it and let loose all the elements. Greed breaks windbag and in so doing destroys Aeolus's protection.

Pppffff, snorted Professor Jones.

Let the wind speak, said A, in the Aeolian dialect.

I think we're going too far. Let the Cicerone go on, B said. Let's not interrupt him any more.

The Cicerone shook his head doubtfully and smoothed his moustache with his forefinger.

8. The Laestrygonians

Ulysses' eleven ships reach the land of the Laestrygonians, man-eating giants who snatch two sailors and throw rocks at the ships from the cliff-tops. Only Ulysses' ship, which he kept wisely out of reach, escapes unscathed.

9. Scylla and Charybdis

Ulysses' ship has to pass between the six-headed monster Scylla and the whirlpool Charybdis. Ulysses steers close to Scylla, which devours six of his men, but he succeeds in avoiding the fatal whirlpool and certain shipwreck.

10. The Wandering Rocks

Ulysses had chosen to steer between Scylla and Charybdis to avoid the even more terrible wandering, or "roving," rocks. Only the *Argo*, the ship of the Argonauts, had successfully navigated between them.

11. The Sirens

Aware that no man can resist the fatal songs of the Sirens, Ulysses plugs his men's ears with beeswax and orders them to tie him to the mast, so that he can hear the enchanting music without danger, while his ship continues on its way.

12. The Cyclops

Ulysses and his crew land on the island of the Cyclops, giant cannibals who each have a single eye. Imprisoned in the cave of one of their number, Polyphemus, they finally manage to escape after Ulysses gets him drunk and drives a red-hot stake into his eye. Furious, the Cyclops hurls rocks at the fleeing ship.

13. Nausicaa

After abandoning the nymph Calypso, Ulysses is shipwrecked once more, but is able to reach the land of the Phaeacians on a plank of wood. He is found unconscious and naked on the shore by the nymph Nausicaa, who was playing ball there with her servants.

14. The Oxen of the Sun

Ulysses tells the Phaeacian court how, after sailing past Scylla and Charybdis, his ships reached the island of the god Helios at nightfall. There, despite Ulysses' warnings, his men killed several cattle from the divine herd and feasted on them for six days. On the seventh they put out to sea, and suffered a terrible fate: Zeus destroyed the ship and all its crew with a thunderbolt. Only Ulysses survived.

After escaping from the jaws of the Laestrygonians, Ulysses and his men end up on the island of the sorceress Circe. She changes them all into swine, except for the cunning Ulysses, who is protected by the magic herb "moly" (remember the name) given him by Hermes. Ulysses spends a year trapped by the embraces and charms of Circe.

PART THREE, OR NOSTOS

After Ulysses has told Alcinous and his court the story of Circe and his earlier misfortunes, he is finally led back to his homeland on a Phaeacian ship. Disguised by Athena as an old beggar, Ulysses appears before his faithful swineherd Eumaeus, who tells him everything that has happened during his absence. Shortly afterwards, Ulysses reveals his true identity to the swineherd and Telemachus.

Disguised as a beggar, Ulysses tricks his way into his palace where the suitors are feasting. As a last resort, Penelope has ordered that there should be an archery competition using Ulysses' bow. The winner of the competition will also win her hand. Only

Ulysses can string the bow, and with the aid of Telemachus and Eumaeus he kills all the suitors, who number no less than one hundred and eight.

18. Penelope

Ulysses reveals his true identity to his faithful, patient Penelope. To remove all traces of doubt, he describes the frame of their marriage bed, since only the two of them know that one of the legs is a living olive tree. The pair withdraw to test the stability of their bed once more and to tell each other all their past misfortunes.

Because of its narrative drive and even its suspense, said C, Homer's poem has rightly been called the first novel.

Its modernity is also remarkable, A said. For example, the use it makes of parallel plotlines and flashbacks.

And what in French is called *mise en abyme*, C said. The story within a story, such as when in the Phaeacian court Ulysses is so moved when he hears his own story sung by the bard Demodocus.

I prefer to return to Joyce's *Ulysses*, said B, or rather to Leopold Bloom, the Wandering Jew of Dublin.

Bloom Ulysses, Sinbad, and Wandering Jew, said A. Three in one.

It's that one, that unique being from Dublin, who interests me, said B. Leopold Bloom, not Odysseus transposed.

They both count, C said. You can tell from the Homeric titles Joyce gave to the chapters of *Ulysses* as they were published in different magazines.

Don't forget though that in the end, B replied impetuously, when he published the complete novel, Joyce decided to get rid of those titles.

He got rid of the chapter titles, said C, but he kept the title of the novel. And the title is key, the first key to the novel.

And we have to bear in mind, A said, that one of the definitions Joyce gave of his *Ulysses* was precisely that of "a modern *Odyssey*."

Yes, said C. Ulysses lives in Dublin in the guise of a foreigner in his own land by the name of Leopold Bloom. In addition, the different Homeric episodes and the overall structure of the *Odyssey* provided the stimulus and the *contrainte*—in the Oulipian sense of the word—as well as helping him establish his own rules in a book that was set to demolish the conventions of the moth-eaten realist novel.

Even the newest inventions, said A, run the risk of eventually becoming conventions . . .

Joyce himself once declared he was worried he had perhaps systematized his novel too much, said C. But after endless critical sifting and the closest study of the entire paraphernalia of outlines, symbols, techniques, and so on, it appears sufficiently clear that chance also played a hand in the composition of *Ulysses*. It does not always follow predetermined patterns, because—like so many artists—Joyce behaved as a true *bricoleur* and used whatever was closest to hand or what chance offered him to construct his novel.

I'm not concerned about how systematic Joyce may have been in writing his novel, A said, but about the more or less delirious systems (every man must have his mania) some readers have applied to it.

Especially when they start distributing kidneys, lungs, esophagi, and other offal through the different chapters of *Ulysses*, said B, grimacing with disgust.

But Joyce himself defined *Ulysses* as an "epic of the human body." The body is the structure underpinning the entire book.

An underpinning pinned to reason, A said. The "metaphysical structures" of theosophy, spiritualism, and all the other mystical mystifications nimbed with gilded or tinsel legends born of the so-called Irish Renaissance met a physical end in Joyce: the presence of the human body. The body and its functions have a function. And to each hour its organ . . .

At ten o'clock sharp, for example, said B sharply, it is the genitals.

In this respect it's significant that it is only in those episodes of the "Telemachia," where the intellectual Stephen Dedalus is the center of attention, that there is no presiding organ, A said.

No, said C., because as Joyce observed: "Telemachus does not yet bear a body."

Or enjoy it, A said.

He is pure word, said C, not yet made flesh. Even his view of women is an idealistic, unrealistic one. It takes the appearance of Leopold Bloom, the "average sensual man," for the body—that of man and of woman—to become present.

To be present and to be offered as present, said A, winking at B.

By attributing a human organ to each chapter, Professor Jones interrupted, Joyce was offering the *disiecti membra poetae*, the scattered limbs that the reader-Isis is to reunite in communion with the author: *this is my corpus*, says the novel, a mystic and at the same time mythic body, like that of HCE in *Finnegans Wake*.

Hero Cum Eucharist, A said.

The Eucharist, said C, is one of the main themes of *Ulysses*.

This is my body, B smiled mischievously, and Don Poldo de la Flora offers us his withered flower in the bath . . .

Chalice and corollary, A began. As far away from me as possible . . .

But the Cicerone frowned at them, and waved his wand at the flashing computer screen:

	ULYSSES I.1.doc	
TITLE: Telemachus	**TECHNIQUE:** Narrative (young), interior monologue, dialogue	
SETTING: The Martello tower	**MEANING:** The dispossessed heir fighting for his rights	
TIME: 8:00–8:45 A.M.	**CORRESPONDENCES:**	
	Telemachus, Hamlet, Faust, and Christ: Stephen	
SCIENCE, ART: Theology	Antinous, Claudius, and Mephistopheles: Buck Mulligan	
	Mentor and Athena: The dairymaid	
SYMBOL: The heir		
COLOR: White, gold		

PART ONE

1. TELEMACHUS

Introit or introduction to the parody-mass: I will approach the altar of the Lord: *Introibo ad altare Dei*, said the Cicerone, hands held high as he imitated the plump, ruddy-faced medical student Malachi ("Buck") Mulligan, who in his dressing gown mockingly raises high his chalice-shaving bowl full of lather before going out onto the parapet to bless sea and sky in turn. The Cicerone then pointed his wand first toward the round tower that dominated Kingstown in the distance, then at a showcase displaying a silver-plated fob watch (It must be Buck Mulligan's, said A), pointing out that it is eight o'clock on Thursday, June 16, 1904 at the Martello tower of Sandycove Point, a rocky promontory on the coast seven miles southeast of Dublin. Take a good look at this bowl, or shaving basin as we might call it, remembering our Quixote (It's already lost its nickel coating, B said), with the cracked mirror and barber's razor that Mulligan raises crossed to start his . . . *mass-en-scène*.

Cross and sword, said A. Irish glass and a barber's razor to begin the sacrifice. His solemn mass . . .

The first and last letter, Professor Jones interrupted them, drawing a twisting capital *S* in the air with his finger. Ulysses begins and ends with an *S*.

Yessss, we agreed.

And the first word of the novel, "Stately," which is to say imposing or solemn, also contains the final "Yes," the three letters inverted.

Yessss, we averred.

Stately, the imposing Professor Jones continued solemnly. But is it an adjective or an adverb: are we meant to read it as solemn or solemn*ly*? Then again, that sibilant first *S* is also the first initial of the main character here . . .

Yessss . . .

Silence! somebody said, and the Cicerone moved on through the white and gold room, explaining the characteristics of those barrel-shaped Martello towers, about twelve meters high and with two-and-a-half meter thick stone walls, which the English scattered round Dublin and the coasts of Ireland to defend against a possible Napoleonic invasion in support of rebels seeking Irish independence. According to the Cicerone, the Martello tower at Sandycove was at this time a century old. The order for it to be built had been given on June 16, 1804—exactly one hundred years earlier.

Did Joyce know the date? asked C.

It was enough for him to be well aware, said A, of the date when he first really ventured into the labyrinth of love with the chambermaid at Finn's Hotel.

His body- and soul-mate, B said. Nora.

The date of his first meeting with Nora Barnacle remains fixed forever, said A.

Since the publication of *Ulysses*, said C, it is better known as "Bloomsday."

The day of Bloom, but also rather close to "Doomsday," the Day of Judgment.

Judgment upon a whole era, said C.

In the tower of *Ulysses* at that time, there lived three young men, the Cicerone explained. Two Irishmen and one Englishman. Buck Mulligan, whom I have already mentioned; a student friend of Mulligan's from Oxford, Haines, who is on a field trip to Dublin to study the local folklore and practice his booklearned Irish; and the apprentice poet and schoolteacher from Dublin, Stephen Dedalus, who is twenty-two years old and is the main character in this first part of *Ulysses*, the "Telemachia," just as he was of Joyce's first novel, *A Portrait of the Artist as a Young Man*.

I always imagine him as the artist portrays him here, B said. With a long sharp face . . .

Sharp as a knife, said C. That's Mulligan's nickname for him: "Kinch, the knife-blade."*

---

* *Kinch*, wrote Professor Jones in his notebook, onomatopoeia for the sound of a knife-blade and a diminutive of *kinchin*, old slang for "little boy."

The stylized aesthete, said A, smiling at the Cicerone, with his bitter new stiletto.

Stephen is still in mourning, B observed, although there are only ten days till the first anniversary of his mother's death.

This is why he refuses the pair of gray trousers Mulligan wants to lend him, said A. The ethics of etiquette.

He finds it easier to obey the strict social codes than he did his mother's last request, said C. She implored him on her deathbed to kneel and say a prayer for her.

Such a cruel refusal, said B. I'm not surprised that even the churlish Mulligan reproached him for it. Apparently Joyce himself had refused to kneel and pray at his dying mother's bedside.

The reality was rather less dramatic, said A. She was already in a coma when their uncle asked Joyce and his brother Stanislaus to pray, and they refused.

What fanatics, B exclaimed.

Like Stephen, said A with conviction, Joyce did not want to pay lip service to things he no longer believed in—whether it was religion, patriotism, or the Holy Family.

There is something of Lucifer in his *Non serviam*, said C. Stephen is also the rebel angel.

Something of Hamlet too, said B, in his dusty mourning. He has the appearance of a gloomy prince.

Yes, a little more than kin, A conceded, drawing a line in the air.

Haines himself says the Martello tower reminds him of Elsinore and Hamlet's castle.

Stephen Hamlet in search of his ghostly father, A added theatrically.

And trying to escape from the ghost of his mother, said Professor Jones. A castrating figure, who even after her death goes on biting and biting in the flow of her son's consciousness: "Agenbite of inwit," to use the term in a medieval missal mentioned by Stephen. She returns, pale vampire in her shroud, holding up her bloody fingernails.

The Red Badge of Mother Courage . . . A said.

The poor woman, said B, reading out: "Her shapely fingernails reddened by the blood of squashed lice from the children's shirts."

She appears to him in nightmares, said Professor Jones. He even comes to beg her: "No, mother! Let me be and let me live."

Stephen the orphan steeped in remorse . . . said A.

Yes, orphaned by his mother and almost by his father, Professor Jones continued. Stephen chasing the image or *imago* of an ideal father to compensate for the failings of his flesh-and-blood father, the wastrel Simon Dedalus.

Stephen is a persona or mask of Joyce, said C. A fairly accurate representation of the young Joyce.

He is also the author of *Dubliners*, said A, and a heteronym of Joyce's. At least, Joyce published some of the *Dubliners* stories under the pseudonym of "Stephen Dedalus."

Apart from the parallels with the *Odyssey* and other works of literature such as *Hamlet* or even *Faust*, said C, there are many autobiographical references in *Ulysses*, literary transfers of the author's own experiences.

Are you saying we should read *Ulysses* with Joyce's biography in our other hand? B asked in alarm.

No doubt about it, young lady, Professor Jones declared roundly. Life and work are doubly intertwined in the great Dubliner. Joyce said, hyperbolically no doubt, that he had no imagination. All he had to do was commend himself to the mother of the Muses and remember . . .

And transpose, said A, because the lines of his life and those of his work are not exactly the same.

But we have to read the palimpsest, said Professor Jones, even if the words are faint and in pale . . .

Fire, said B. I still prefer the lecture Professor Nabokov gave in his class on *Ulysses*, wherein he dismissed Joyce's entire life in three lines. I know them *par coeur*: "James Joyce was born in 1882 in Ireland, he left Ireland in the first decade of the twentieth century, lived most of his life as an expatriate in continental Europe, and died in 1941 in Switzerland."

Life is short, said A, extending his arms, for such a long art.

In order more fully to understand this first chapter, said the Cicerone, we should bear in mind details and experiences shared by Stephen Dedalus and his creator James Joyce. In 1904 both are of the same age—twenty-two years old. They come from similar families, they have both studied at Jesuit schools and at University College Dublin, and both went to Paris for a while, intending to study medicine, but had to come back suddenly because their mothers (Mary Goulding and Mary Jane Murray, respectively) were gravely ill—the first dying on June 26, the second on August 13, 1903 . . . both of cancer.

A beastly way to go, as the beastly Mulligan said, B reminded us.

The very man who is now showing his white teeth, or their edges, still covered in lather ("That whited sepulcher . . ." said A), next to the man he calls "Toothless," said the Cicerone, in front of the mirror in which Mulligan and Stephen are partly reflected.

Chrysostomos, A murmured. Golden teeth, golden-mouthed orator . . .

The first word in Stephen's interior monologue, "Chrysostomos," refers both to Mulligan's skills as an orator and to his gold-capped teeth, but it gains still more meaning if we remember that the real-life model for Mulligan was Oliver *St. John* Gogarty, said the Cicerone, a live-wire, Rabelaisian medical student (who afterwards became a surgeon, politician, and publicist, and was a well-known Dublin character), a friend of Joyce's in his youth, whom he lived with for a few days, from September 9 to 15, 1904, in the same Martello tower of the novel. And the prototype for Haines, Mulligan's English friend, was Samuel Chenevix Trench, scion of a distinguished Anglo-Irish family. His nightmare about a black panther that so frightened Stephen was even blacker and more disturbing in real life than in fiction: Trench fired his revolver to drive away the dreadful night panther, and shortly afterwards Gogarty also shot at some pans hanging above Joyce's bed, forcing him to leave the tower in the early hours, never to set foot in the place again. Since 1962, the Martello tower has been the James Joyce Museum, but paradoxically it was, until 1925 at least, still Gogarty's tower, because it was he, unlike the opportunist Mulligan, who paid the rent. It was eight pounds a year rather than the twelve in the novel, and Joyce surely remembered that the rental agreement was signed by one Colonel Haynes, on behalf of the British Ministry of Defence, the owners of the disused fortification.

The name "Haines" suggests "hatreds" in French, said Professor Jones, perhaps because of the character's anti-Semitism.

Perhaps the hatreds were in Stephen, said A. Haines represented everything he detested: English domination and folkloric Gaelic nationalism.

His *bêtes noires,* said C.

And the dream of the black panther is a premonition. The panther prefigures Leopold Bloom. Professor Jones was close to roaring: What's in a name? LEOpold is feline, just as Stephen is canine. "Dogsbody," Mulligan calls him.

It also means servile, said C.

A vile sir? Asked B.

Vile is evil as dog is God. The body of God: *Godsbody*? asked A.

Don't forget, said Professor Jones, that in medieval bestiaries the panther was an emblem of Christ. In those days people thought it was a tame animal whose only enemy was the dragon.

Later however it became a symbol for hypocrisy and evil, said A. From pantheism to pander.

Professor Jones would not be denied:

It could also be argued that the panther represents the Antichrist, to say nothing of the Talmudic legend which maintains that Jesus descended from a Roman legionary by the name of Pandera.

Nightmares gallop away in the dark, B said. Let the panther vanish like smoke.

No smoke without firearms, said A, raising his forefinger to his temple. One more shot and I'll be off.

In fact, their friendship had ended before the shooting started, when Gogarty used the same words as Mulligan about Joyce's mother being "beastly dead." Joyce never forgot or forgave that expression. Here we see him, said the Cicerone, leaning on the parapet submerged in doubts, remorse gnawing at his conscience—as frayed and black as his sleeve—still bothered by the offense he thought was aimed at him—and not his mother!—by the materialist Gogarty, who was so used to autopsies at the Mater Hospital that for him the dead body of a person was no better than that of a dog. Across the frayed edges of his cuff and his memory there is a fusion, in one of the sublime passages of *Ulysses*, between the sea and his mother ("a great sweet mother," Mulligan calls it, mockingly paraphrasing Swinburne), the jagged parapet with Mulligan's shaving mug and the china bowl where his mother vomited, and the snot-green ring of the bay (also the color of Stephen's dirty handkerchief) and the "green sluggish bile" of his mother's "rotting liver."

From the platform Mulligan and Stephen could see the sleeping whale's snout of Bray Head in the distance, although in reality the view of it is obscured by a hill, B pointed out.

On a clear day in a dark novel you can see forever, A declared.

It's true you can't see Bray Head, said C. Some experts get terribly worked up about the inaccuracy. Others however point out punctiliously that in fact the novel says the two friends halted and looked "*towards* the blunt cape."

Perhaps we could gloss over the glosses . . . A said.

Look instead at the cloud covering the sun and darkening the dull green mass of the sea, said the Cicerone. We'll see it again at the same time, a few chapters further on, but from a different point of view.

"A bowl of bitter waters," quoted B.

La mer amère . . . said A.

"Love's Bitter Mystery," B sang.

In Stephen's mother, Mary, there are also the Mother Church and the Mother Country, C said.

And the *Stella Maris*, murmured A.

"Look at the sea," said C. That's what Mulligan told Stephen to do.

I can't see what you see in the sea, said A.

Look at the sea, said the Cicerone, quoting Mulligan, it wipes everything away, but Stephen sees another abyss opening beneath him, another mirror for his mother's soul in torment and his own interior hell: a mirror of himself or a mirage? "Look at yourself!" Mulligan had exclaimed shortly before, as if he were telling him to "know thyself," offering him the cracked mirror stolen from the maid's room at his aunt's, which Stephen converts into a symbol of Irish art: "The cracked looking-glass of a servant," a memorable epigram (with the unwitting aid of Oscar Wilde), which the scrounger Mulligan thinks (although Stephen ignores him) they could get a guinea for from the well-off Haines, who is waiting in the domed living room for his breakfast or the continuation of the mass—offertory, consecration, and communion—that the false prelate Mulligan will go on parodying, *In nomine Patris, et Filii, et Spiritus Sancti*, complaining there is no milk until the old milkmaid finally arrives. She is servile, ignorant, and oppressed, the personification of the Irish people, and treats the future Doctor Mulligan with especial deference, allowing him to owe her two pennies, as well as the English "Lord" Haines who deigns to address her in what she takes to be French. This is a particularly comic moment that allows Joyce to ridicule the pretensions of those who support Celtic nationalism in Ireland.

If we continue with the rites, we now come to ablution, A said.

Yes, Mulligan asks Stephen if this is the day for his monthly wash, said B. And he has not had a bath since October. Almost nine months ago!

Which only goes to increase the odor of sanctity about him, said A. Stephen is following the example of a great many saints and anchorites. Besides, as he retorted with the savvy saw that Haines would have liked to add to his collection: "All Ireland is washed by the gulfstream."

But we might also see his dislike of water as a rejection of being baptized, said Professor Jones.

And St. John Gogarty will be his Saint John the Baptist, A said ironically.

Despite his reluctance to bathe, said the Cicerone, Stephen goes with Mulligan and Haines to the rocky cove known as "Forty Foot" down below the tower, a men-only bathing hole where even today brave Dubliners go to bathe naked.

Look, said A, here comes the anointed priest leaving the water . . .

It's a very significant image, the Cicerone explained, that we need to examine closely. To begin with, we are not told that he is a priest, but Mulligan shows it when he crosses himself as the old man in the loincloth passes by.

He's the only bather who is not naked, said B, and he hides to get dressed.

He represents the prudishness and sanctimoniousness that Stephen is trying to leave behind him, C said.

"I will not sleep here tonight," read B. "Home also I cannot go."

When he leaves his fake friend, the fake priest and fake artist Mulligan (Even his teeth are false, said B), Stephen also leaves behind the tower, a symbol of English domination just as Haines is, our Cicerone concluded. But before going he leaves the two pennies Mulligan had asked him for to buy a pint of beer, and the key to the tower.

And so keyless Stephen sets off for his encounter with someone who has no key to his house either, said C.

As he heads off towards the school, Stephen looks back from a bend at Mulligan's seal head in the water, said the Cicerone. A metamorphosis that underlines Buck Mulligan's animal nature.

Buck, or messenger of the gods, Professor Jones explained. That is what Malachi means in Hebrew, a messenger like Hermes for the Greeks, here transformed into a seal, an animal consecrated to Poseidon, Ulysses' sworn enemy.

Let us simply listen to the last word of the chapter, aimed at Mulligan (Antinous/Claudius) from the mind of Stephen (Telemachus/Hamlet): "Usurper."

Passageways

I

Here we have the mirror and the razor, crossed on top of the ba-sin-chalice overflowing with lather or white corpuscles, according to Mulligan's sacrilegious transubstantiation, as the Cicerone explained.

The razor of *Kinch, the knife-blade*, said A, that will cut a *slice of life*, reflected in the cracked mirror of Irish art.

The razor is also the instrument of sacrifice, Professor Jones concluded, and the scalpel that Mulligan the medical student wields.

II

The "mild morning air," B recalled, gently blew the dressing gown that Mulligan was wearing untied.

The yellow of Mulligan's dressing gown suggests the liturgical gold of June 16, said Professor Jones professorially, but it is also the color of betrayal and heresy. Judas is frequently portrayed in yellow garments, and in autos-da-fé heretics had to wear a yellow gown.

III

The dirty, crumpled handkerchief that Mulligan takes from Stephen's pocket to wipe his razor with, indicated the Cicerone.

Mulligan was immediately interested in local color, said A.

"The bard's noserag!" read B. "A new art colour for our Irish poets: snotgreen. You can almost taste it, can't you?"

Green snot, how green I love you, A mucously mocked. Snot as the concretion and excretion of Irish phlegm . . .

IV

The image of the soapy face reflected in the looking glass brings together several moments in the first chapter, the Cicerone explained, both before and after Mulligan's shave. His plump cheeks and oval jowls recall a medieval prelate.

Mulligan's guffaw, giving a glimpse of gold, said A, and added: Chrysostomos.

Mulligan then hands Stephen the cracked mirror so that he can see himself as others see him, said the Cicerone.

The mirror of a servant girl, said Professor Jones, which Stephen scornfully sees as a symbol of Irish art.

The mirror robbed from a skivvy, B concluded.

V

The bay-bowl . . . A said.

B read:

"The ring of bay and skyline held a dull green mass of liquid. A bowl of white china had stood beside her deathbed holding the green sluggish bile which she had torn up from her rotting liver by fits of loud groaning vomiting."

Stephen drinks the contents of the chalice to the dregs, said A.

VI

The old milkmaid who to Stephen seems like the personification of Ireland in its many contradictory aspects, said the Cicerone. In the hallucinatory "Circe" episode, she appears as the devouring mother, as she was already described in *A Portrait of the Artist*; a description that is repeated in *Ulysses*: Ireland is "the old sow that eats her farrow."

VII

Watch out for the significant detail, the Cicerone warned us as B began to read to us by candlelight:

"Haines stopped to take out a smooth silver case in which twinkled a green stone. He sprang it open with his thumb and offered it.

– Thank you, Stephen said, taking a cigarette.

Haines helped himself and snapped the case to."

The *petit-maître*, or dandy . . . said A.

C pointed with his pipe:

The Emerald Isle set in his cigarette case.

Ireland his joke or his jewel . . . A concluded.

ERIN, GREEN GEM OF THE SILVER SEA.

VIII

The key to the Martello tower and two pennies on a pile of clothes, said the Cicerone. Buck Mulligan asks Stephen for the key to keep his shirt flat and then asks him for the two pennies for a pint.

B suddenly realized:

He could have used those two pennies to settle the debt with the poor dairymaid.

2. NESTOR

On the screen you can now see—and the Cicerone pointed his pointer at the Macintosh and its man—the outline corresponding to the second episode in the "Telemachia":

TITLE: Nestor

SETTING: The school

TIME: 9:40–10:05 A.M.

SCIENCE, ART: History

SYMBOL: The horse

COLOR: Brown

TECHNIQUE: Catechism (personal), narration, dialogue, interior monologue

MEANING: The wisdom of the ancient world

CORRESPONDENCES:
Nestor: Mr. Deasy
Pisistratus (Nestor's youngest son): Sargent
Elena: Mrs. O'Shea (Parnell's lover)
Telemachus: Stephen

Stephen is giving his history lesson (with additional elements of literature and math), in a private school in the residential suburb of Dalkey, a mile south of the Martello tower. The school takes in boys from well-off Anglo-Irish and British families, and is run by the ancient Mr. Deasy, the novel's garrulous Nestor.

Since it is Thursday it is half-day at the school, and the lack of interest shown by both teacher and pupils shows they are more concerned with the coming break-time (which is at ten o'clock) than with the lesson.

Stephen's first questions to the boys are about Pyrrhus, and these give rise to various versions and diversions.

We also had to reply, thanks in the main to the three readers, our "ABC of *Ulysses*," and Professor Jones, to the questions the Cicerone occasionally fired at us.

Pyrrhus, sir? Pyrrhus, the king of Epirus, the one made famous by his Pyrrhic victory, which term could also be applied to the high cost of Stephen's efforts—but the name also alludes to Achilles' son, nicknamed Pyrrhus, whose happy return from Troy is told of by Nestor in the *Odyssey*. This doubling-up is a constant in Joyce. In the same way, a Vico Road appears between the two Pyrrhuses, which helps maintain the ambiguity.

Vico, sir? Thanks to the device of bringing Vico's name into the equation, Stephen scores a double hit: he mentions a street in Dalkey where one of his pupils, Armstrong, lives, showing that he comes from a comfortable social background, while at the same time bringing in the name of the great philosopher of history, the theme of this chapter.

As always in Joyce, this Vico Road takes us from the specific to the general, said C.

Although Giambattista Vico (1668–1744) plays a vital role in the structure of *Finnegans Wake*, Professor Jones explained, his presence was already to be felt in the *Portrait*, and even more significantly in *Ulysses*. At first sight, the notion of history on which this chapter is based seems closer to that of the philosopher and theosophist Giordano Bruno, burned at the stake as a heretic in 1600, and the English visionary poet William Blake, who provides us with the first apocalyptic image of this episode ("I hear the ruin of all space, shattered glass and toppling masonry, and time one livid final flame," B read), and the first indication of the *this is how history is written* that underpins the whole chapter, Stephen using Blake's words to refer to the notion that history is mere story or fiction, a fable of the Muses; despite this, Vico's concept of history is the invisible foundation supporting the three chapters of the first part, the "Telemachia," of *Ulysses*—the theocratic, aristocratic, and democratic stages.

The aristocratic stage in this second chapter is signaled by the exclusive nature of the school and the frequent mention of kings and heroes.

To return to something more concrete, said B, I love the scene where Stephen secretly looks in his history book for the place and date of the Pyrrhic battle that he has just asked his pupil, Cochrane, to provide.

It's a filthy book, A said, with stains that suggest the brown of dirt and dried blood—*gorescarred*, it says.

The brown color that this chapter is steeped in comes not only from the dried blood of history, said the Cicerone, but also from the leather of the old chairs in Mr. Deasy's study and the brown of the horses in the paintings on the study walls.

Houyhnhnm! snorted Professor Jones. The symbol of this chapter is the horse, and Mr. Deasy's passion for racehorses mirrors Nestor the horse-tamer.

The past is always browned off, said A. As you can see from old photos and documents.

But it is also the color of the bog that the history of Ireland is forever sinking into, said Professor Jones.

The past passes the pupils by. They ask Stephen to tell them a ghost story, but in the end he tells them a riddle, the Cicerone told us:

> *The cock crew,*
> *The sky was blue:*
> *The bells in heaven*
> *Were striking eleven.*
> *'Tis time for this poor soul*
> *To go to heaven.*

What's the answer, sir?

"The fox burying his grandmother under a hollybush," according to Stephen. It's an absurd riddle that Stephen adapted from a book by another Joyce, *English as We Speak It in Ireland* (1910) by P. W. Joyce. There, however, the fox was burying his *mother.* Stephen's alteration is significant, and his nervous laughter and sense of guilt are understandable. Stephen the fox constantly digging up his mother in his memory. In fact, as A said, you have to become a son—Stephen—for the riddle to make any sense. Then again, the eleven o'clock in the riddle acts as a memento mori, because at eleven that same morning it will be Patrick Dignam's funeral, which we will be present at in chapter six of the book. By using the word "grandmother," Stephen is also trying to bury all the burdens of history—the "nightmare" from which he is "trying to awaken," as one of his most brilliant aphorisms (in collaboration with Jules Laforgue) tells us: that multiple nightmare which includes his phantom mother, Ireland with its battles, betrayals, and famines, an intolerant Church, and a crumbling British Empire . . . all of which combine in his own past and become present once more in the figure of the shortsighted, clumsy, and ungainly Sargent, who (after his classmates have run off to play hockey) comes to ask for help with his algebra, and who seems to Stephen like the spitting image of himself as a boy coddled by his mother.

Following this, Stephen enters the almost antique-shop study of the antique Mr. Deasy. He is given his pay—three pounds and twelve shillings—as well as the advice and warnings of a highly prejudiced "Nestor," a convinced Anglophile, conservative, misogynist, anti-Semite, and, worst of all, himself unsure of the historical dates and most of the other information he so smugly imparts, such as, for example, that Ireland never persecuted the Jews because it never let them in; finally putting his foot in it by lumbering Stephen with a letter on foot-and-mouth disease—a "footnote"—which he wants him to try to get published in the newspapers.

Mr. Deasy, with his theocratic idea of history and his loyalty to the British Empire, as represented by the portrait of Edward VII on his wall, represents the fusion of the first two cycles of history as Vico saw it, said Professor Jones. Stephen responds to this theocentric view of history, whose goal is the manifestation of God, with his democratic "shout in the street."

"That is God . . . A shout in the street," B remembered.

Perhaps with this mysterious maxim, Stephen is paraphrasing another from the Book of Proverbs, the Cicerone hazarded. The book of books that is *Ulysses* is filled with enigmas and riddles. We have already seen some of them in this chapter. At any rate, by the end of this class, Stephen has learned who is the great teacher.

History? B asked.

Who, sir?*

---

* That's life.

Passageways

I

They all burst out laughing, said the Cicerone, when one of Stephen's pupils tells him Pyrrhus was a *pier*.

A pyrrhic pirouette that gives Stephen an empirical victory over the dock of the bay, said A.

Encore "pier," said B the Francophone.

II

A bridge . . . B started to say.

Too far? A interrupted her.

"A disappointed bridge," B quoted.

Yes, a frustrated bridge, Professor Jones pontificated. That is Stephen's brilliant definition of a pier. Another aphorism for Haines's chapbook. The pier also represents Stephen's as yet unfulfilled desire to leave.

In fact, Stephen was referring to a specific pier, ruled the Cicerone. Stephen says that the Kingstown pier is a *disappointed* or frustrated bridge, cut off in its prime. The port of Kingstown (now called Dún Laoghaire) is protected by two long breakwaters. In Stephen's day, the East Pier, almost a mile long, was a popular promenade. A promenade leading to nowhere, because it was cut off by the sea.

III

It is worth listening to Stephen's monologue when he sees Sargent's face before him, with the fresh ink-stain on it . . . said the Cicerone.

The squire of doleful countenance, A said.

A date-shaped stain, to be precise, C recalled.

At a nod from C, B began to read to us:

> Ugly and futile: lean neck and tangled hair and a stain of ink, a snail's bed. Yet someone had loved him, borne him in her arms and in her heart. But for her the race of the world would have trampled him underfoot, a squashed boneless snail. She had loved his weak watery blood drained from her own. Was that then real? The only true thing in life?

Amor matris, said C, the only true thing in life.

Subjective and objective genitive, A said.

IV

Stephen helps Sargent do his sums, the Cicerone explained, but he hasn't got his own in order, and has not resolved the complicated algebraic problem set out in the first chapter, proving that Shakespeare's ghost is Hamlet's grandfather.

Stephen's problem is in the mind, it's internal, said C.

His internal problem is his *Inferno*. Is hell oneself? asked A.

Please don't keep going round in circles, C begged him.

And B, as if deciphering Arabic numbers, began to read:

> Across the page the symbols moved in grave morrice, in the mummery of their letters, wearing quaint caps of squares and cubes. Give hands, traverse, bow to partner: so: imps of fancy of the Moors.

V

We are in Mr. Deasy's dusty study, said the Cicerone, looking at the portrait of the Prince of Wales in his kilt above the mantelpiece.

The old curiosity shop of history, said A. With its tray of Stuart coins, apostle spoons, shells.

The best moment comes, said B, when Stephen moves his hand over a scallop shell.

He worships the shell of Saint James, said A. It is his scallop Santiago.

Mr. Deasy goes over to his desk, said the Cicerone, to finish typing the letter on foot-and-mouth disease that is going to be so useful to Stephen in the next chapter.

VI

Stephen calls the lions on the gate pillars "toothless terrors" as he leaves Mr. Deasy's school, the Cicerone pointed out.

3. PROTEUS

"Ineluctable modality of the visible": snotgreen (of seaspawn and seawrack), bluesilver (the polished surface of the sea), rust (an old boot on the shore), tidemarks (rising), colored signs, the signatures of things (a few steps farther on, a half-buried bottle of beer, broken hoops from a barrel, the keel of a rowboat) that we too can read in the page of sand while Stephen prowls the beach of his mind.

(With the help of Aristotle, past master at this sort of thing, and even the alchemist and mystic Jacob Boehme—the boot is now on the other foot—and Bishop Berkeley.)

Stephen walks along the beach at Sandymount for half an hour, south of the estuary of the River Liffey and nine miles from Dominie Deasy's school, reflecting and remembering on the rocky road to Dublin.

Green sea and emerald green Erin, and Stephen's oval epiphanies—how to really see—on this screen that now brightens again:

TITLE: Proteus	TECHNIQUE: Monologue (male)
SETTING: Sandymount Strand	MEANING: Raw material (Protean) and the ever-changing flux of the mind
TIME: 10:40–11:10 A.M.	
	CORRESPONDENCES:
SCIENCE, ART: Philology	Proteus: The sea
	Menelaus: Kevin Egan
SYMBOL: The tide	
COLOR: Green	

Stephen closes his eyes and feels his way with his ash cane.

"Ineluctable modality of the audible . . . crush, crack, crick . . ." Stephen walks with closed eyes into eternity along the strand at Sandymount, crushing shells, pebbles, seaweed beneath his secondhand—or as Mulligan would say, second-foot—boots. Crack.

He opens his eyes and sees. Does he stumble?

"There all the time without you: and ever shall be, world without end."

(Stephen the solipsist succeeds in peering out: the world is real, and exists independently of our perception. Aristotle's sconce or Dr. Johnson's kick smashing the sophisticated idealism of Berkeley to smithereens . . .)

It could be said that Stephen is here finally brought into the world because the first thing he sees when he opens his eyes are the two midwives (or what he thinks of as midwives) climbing down the steps of the promenade wall to the beach. "One of her sisterhood lugged me squealing into life," he reflects.

After this he once again summons his mother-phantom, "with ashes on her breath," who bore him in her womb. And he sees himself four months earlier in Paris, with his Latin Quarter hat ("Hat, tie, overcoat, nose," the police or identikit portrait of his guilty Parisian alter ego), living a carefree bohemian student life until a telegram arrived, with a typo, *Nother dying come home father*, forcing him to return to a family and a country in ruins, although he still rebels against them as he walks along the beach, and makes a detour but in the end does not visit his aunt and uncle Sara and Richie Goulding.

Stephen links his rebelliousness with the figure of the exiled nationalist Kevin Egan, whom he met in Paris, someone completely forgotten in Ireland. Stephen too feels like a pariah in his own land. A "poor dogsbody," as Mulligan calls him, suddenly presents itself in the swollen carcass of a dead dog among the seaweed, and then comes back to life again in the moving and changing image of two gypsies gathering cockles on the beach.

Stephen recalls Haines's nightmare ("the panthersahib") and history once more ("Famine, plague and slaughters"), but also his previous night's dream (in a street of harlots, an oriental gentleman, Haroun al Raschid, offers him a succulent, perfumed melon . . .), which by the end of the novel will be revealed as a premonition.

A few chapters further on in the book, on this same beach, a Jewish Ulysses will indulge in solitary pleasure at the sight of a Dublin Nausicaa, who reveals to him her most intimate charms.

Is reading Stephen's only solitary pleasure? Stephen is on the beach to read: "These heavy sands are language tide and wind have silted here." These sands are also the sands of the past. Philology—the science dominating this chapter—and reading give way to romantic delectation. Brought on by the activity of reading. Stephen is not on the beach simply to read.

Sitting on a rock next to the sea, he writes on the only piece of paper he can find—part of Mr. Deasy's letter—verses about vampiric kisses that reveal his filial necrophilia.

Stephen on the rocky road? Also tempted by the solitary pleasure or self-service that will be enjoyed by, shall we say, his putative father. Keeping his hand in could give rise to a scandalous interpretation.

"Touch me. Soft eyes. Soft soft soft hand. I am lonely here. O, touch me soon, now."

And then the riddle constantly posed throughout *Ulysses*: "What is that word known to all men?"* followed by the toccata as he lies flat on the rocks:

"I am quiet here alone. Sad too. Touch, touch me."

It begins to cloud over. Stephen gets up and goes on a pilgrimage into his own country with his "cockle hat and staff," heading for the "evening lands"—the labyrinth of Dublin—when the three masts of a ship appear on the horizon.

---

* Oh, godly guessing game:
    God! said B.
    Yes and no, said C. He's still searching for the precise word.

Passageways

I

That rusty boot . . .

Real booty among the flotsam fettering Stephen's eyes as he wanders along Sandymount Strand.

They are perhaps in a not much better state than the broad, creased castoffs (lent to him by Buck Mulligan) in which Stephen is walking into *externity* . . .

II

The midwife's bag, or the bag of life linking humanity through the shared umbilical—or telephone—cord, in Stephen's mythical call to the origins: "Hello! Kinch here. Put me on to Edenville. Aleph, alpha: nought, nought, one." Creation or birth born from nothing under the protection of the umbrella, or *gamp*, named after the nurse Sarah Gamp in Dickens's novel *The Life and Adventures of Martin Chuzzlewit*. In the end, we all come from the same limited company: the Eden Land Corporation.

III

"Cousin Stephen, you will never be a saint," Stephen tells himself, paraphrasing the observation made by the English poet John Dryden to the Irish satirist Jonathan Swift: "Cousin Swift, you will never be a poet." Stephen—who renounced his religious vocation in *Portrait*—prefers to be a poet on the isle of saints.

In his imagination, he fuses images of the mad Dean Swift, the oval horselike faces of the Houyhnhnms, the false prophet Buck Mulligan, the aged priest at the bathing hole, and a plump priest at the moment of raising the host.

The "dringdring" of bells that no longer ring his bell.

Stephen has decided his place is not in the Church. He has renounced all its pomps and works.

IV

In his soliloquy Stephen asks himself if the darkness is not in our souls. But out of his dark night of the soul he also longs for the light, and walks toward illumination.

"Gold light on sea, on sand, on boulders."

V

The cocklepickers' dog attracts Stephen's attention as he sits alone on his rock. As he watches it digging in the sand he is reminded of the memento mori of the cunning fox burying its grandmother. To complete the list of associations, the dog also becomes a leopard and a panther. In fact, that dog at Sandymount is etymologically a *panther*—that is to say, "all animals." And its metamorphoses (which recall the transformations Proteus undergoes when he faces Menelaus) begin a few moments earlier, when it changes from a hare to a hornless buck, a bear, a wolf . . .

VI

A man's trousers with a woman's shoe peeping out below, said B.

We ought to make a special footnote of that image, which shows a certain fetishism, A said.

Wilde's love that dare not speak its name, Professor Jones suggested, in drag?

Stephen trying on Esther Osvalt's shoe, a girl he knew in Paris, the Cicerone said. "*Tiens, quel petit pied!*"

Cinderella found the shoe fit . . . said A.

VII

Ulysses is a labyrinth of *excreta*, said A. These excretions pile up, and are never hidden. The characters defecate, urinate, and spit like all human beings.

C observed, Perhaps that is what made some delicate writers such as Virginia Woolf turn their noses up at the book.

Did Stephen urinate or masturbate on the beach at Sandymount? asked B.

What we can be certain of, the Cicerone explained, is that after searching his pockets in vain for the handkerchief he had lent Mulligan to clean his razor with, Stephen picked some dry snot from his nostril and carefully placed it on the ledge of a rock.

The offering of a bard, A said, not to be sniffed at . . .

VIII

Schooner ahoy! shouted the Cicerone, and a three-master at that.

The image of Calvary, said Professor Jones. Crossing the bar.

Cross and fiction, said A. Everyone has their cross to bear.

"Her sails brailed up on the crosstrees," as it says in *Ulysses*, is not exactly right in nautical terms, said Professor Jones. But Joyce needed the word *crosstrees* in order to refer to the cross Jesus was crucified on.

But the Cicerone refused to beat about any bush or tree.

As we will discover in episodes ten and sixteen, the schooner was the *Rosevean*, bringing a load of bricks from Bridgewater.

PART TWO

4. CALYPSO

Gutsy Bloom . . . was A's comment after B read us the start of Mr. Bloom's day, revealing how he liked eating "the inner organs of beasts and fowls," for example giblet soup, gizzards, stuffed heart, liver slices, cod's roes, and above all grilled mutton kidneys "which gave to his palate a fine tang of faintly scented urine."

And his mouth started watering at the thought of kidneys, said A, as he glided round the kitchen.

Mmm, mused B.

This second part begins with the M for Molly . . . Professor Jones reminded us.

And for *moly*, the magic herb Hermes gave Ulysses, said C.

We are back at eight o'clock on that gentle June morning, the Cicerone said, showing us into the orange room, and we are at 7 Eccles Street, in the northwest of Dublin: the home of the Bloom family.

It's a respectable address, said C. In those days it was a quiet, middle-class area.

TITLE: Calypso	ORGAN: Kidneys
SETTING: The house	TECHNIQUE: Narrative (mature), dialogue, soliloquy
TIME: 8:00–8:45 A.M.	MEANING: The departing traveler
SCIENCE, ART: Economy	CORRESPONDENCES:
	Calypso: Molly Bloom—"The Nymph"
SYMBOL: The nymph	Ulysses: Leopold Bloom
COLOR: Orange	

Nowadays there's nothing left of the house, sighed the Cicerone, except for the door, which is on display on the wall of the Bailey Pub on Duke Street, somewhere we will be visiting in another four chapters.

Number 7 Eccles Street is another of Joyce's knowing winks, said A. If Ulysses' day commemorates Joyce's definitive meeting with the woman of his life, these details are those of the woman he thought he had lost forever.

The Cicerone was explaining that, according to the Thom Directory, in 1904 the house was empty (someone by the name of Finneran [sic] was living there in 1905, said Professor Jones), but several years later it was inhabited by one of Joyce's closest

Dublin friends: John F. Byrne, who was to play an important role at a crucial moment for the author of *Ulysses* when he visited Dublin in 1909 for the first time since his elopement with Nora five years earlier.

He returned a month later on October 18, 1909, said Professor Jones, to set up Dublin's first cinema with the help of four business backers from Trieste.

But the Volta ran out of volts, said A.

It might be a good idea to mention the cinematographic effects in *Ulysses,* said Professor Jones. He went off to talk to the Cicerone, who was still speaking about Joyce's first return home with his eldest son Giorgio, then aged four, while Nora stayed behind in Trieste to look after their other child, Lucia, who was two. The trip helped Joyce refresh his memory with details that were later incorporated in altered form in *Ulysses.* One of his university colleagues, Vincent Cosgrave (the prototype for Lynch)—possibly encouraged by Mulligan-Gogarty—confessed to Joyce he had also enjoyed "walking out" with Nora in that year of initiation, 1904. This news devastated Joyce (He felt "dishonoured," said A), and he turned up at 7 Eccles Street to cry his heart out over such a dreadful betrayal. Byrne concluded it had all been an "accursed lie," the slander of a disappointed rival, and this was confirmed by Joyce's younger brother, Stanislaus, who "looked after" him in Trieste.

Even so, jealousy and a certain masochism suited Joyce quite well, said Professor Jones. They helped him plot his literary works, as *Ulysses* and his only play *Exiles* potently (or impotently?) demonstrate.

Le cocu magnifié, said A. The Gordian cuckold and the marriage knot . . .

Yes, that is one of the most complex and important aspects of Joyce's work, C said. He broke off *Ulysses* to write *Exiles,* which was a kind of catharsis.

"Catharsis" was the title of a short story that Joyce never completed, Professor Jones pointed out.

After *Exiles,* said A, he could take the subject by the horns and keep it at a distance.

Be that as it may, said C, there was always the shadow of a doubt, or of a Cosgrave . . .

In 1926, Cosgrave, whose occupation was described as "former medical student," was found drowned in London. He may have fallen drunk into the River Thames, or committed suicide, the Cicerone informed us with forensic indifference. He was forty-eight. This seems to be a confirmation of Stephen's prophecy in "Circe" that Lynch would end up killing himself as Judas did.

"*Exit Judas,*" B quoted. "*Et laqueo se suspendit.*"

Lynch lynched himself, said A. Death by water . . .

The drowned man is an important figure and arcanum from the opening chapter of *Ulysses,* Professor Jones assured us, and Cosgrave was not lucky enough to have that great swimmer Gogarty there to save him from drowning. But I'd like to draw your attention as well to the fact that the real-life Haines, Tench (The *panthersahib,* A noted) also ended up committing suicide, blowing his brains out.

Boom . . . booma . . . puma! A shouted, twisting his forefinger against his temple.

The Cicerone seemed more interested in other points of similarity, such as the fact that Joyce made Leopold Bloom the same height (1 meter, 74 centimeters) and the same weight (71 kilos) as Byrne. These and many other details appeared on the screen of the Macintosh, including Bloom's age—thirty-eight—born in Dublin of a Jewish father with Hungarian ancestors, Rudolph Bloom—originally called Virag ("flower" in Hungarian)—and an Irish mother, Helen Higgins. Baptized first as a Protestant and then as a Catholic, currently employed as an advertising agent for the *Freeman* newspaper, married for sixteen years to the soprano Marion ("Molly") Bloom, maiden name Tweedy, with whom he had two children: a daughter, Millicent ("Milly"), recently turned fifteen, a photographer's assistant in the town of Mullingar (Following in the footsteps of one of her grandfather's cousins, someone called Stefan Virag no less, a photography pioneer, said Professor Jones), and a son, Rudolph ("Rudy"), who died on January 9, 1894, eleven days after he was born. Further distinguishing characteristics, said the Cicerone, include Bloom's olive-colored complexion, and the fact that his fish eyes and slicked-back hair are dark. He is beginning to get a paunch and is flat-footed.

And he is uncircumcised, Professor Jones said circumspectly. Also, since November 27, 1893, exactly five weeks before the birth of his son Rudy, he has been unable to fulfill his marital obligations.

For ten years, five months, and eighteen days, B specified.

Get your dates right, Professor Jones corrected her. The catechism of "Ithaca" is not always infallible.

Poor Bloom, B went on, we can hardly say that his blooming waistline is a sign of happiness . . .

Better to keep the secrets of the bedroom under lock and key, said C.

Forgetting the key and the way that Bloom jumps from the railings to the basement of the house in the early hours, which are things Joyce took from Byrne and an incident when they came back together to 7 Eccles Street early one morning, the Cicerone insisted.

Ulysses is not a *roman à clef*, B protested.

It's a *roman à Eccles*, A retorted.

The Book of Eccles, said C. That's how he described *Ulysses* in *Finnegans Wake*: "his usylessly unreadable Blue Book of Eccles."

Ulysible, A exclaimed in Gallic mode.

We have paused to look at Joyce's attack of jealousy, said Professor Jones, because it can offer us a better understanding of this tale of a foretold and accepted act of adultery and the fatalism and masochism that characterize Bloom.

What is most interesting, C added, is that Joyce knew the house in Eccles Street very well, because as we have seen during that anguished month of August in 1909, he went to visit his friend Byrne there on several occasions, and years later he wrote asking his aunt Josephine (one of his regular informers about Dublin) to confirm certain details, such as the number of steps at the entrance.

I think it's more important to find out what the house was like than to dwell on Joyce's jealousy, said B.

To explain what 7 Eccles Street looked like, the Cicerone pointed toward the terrace of Georgian brick houses, with railings at the front, that stretched as far as Dorset Street. The house had three floors (with two windows on each floor) and a basement (the kitchen where we still found ourselves), no hot water or bathroom, with a W.C. on the landing and another in the back garden. The

Blooms live on the first floor. Their bedroom, which looks out over the garden, takes up the second floor at the back of the house. The third floor is empty and is let unfurnished.

I hope you're not going to describe the hallstand for us, said C, impatiently knocking the bowl of his pipe against his palm. Let's get on with the breakfast.

"Another slice of bread and butter," said A. That makes four.

Breakfast is almost ready, said B, licking her lips. Mm.

It's a point in Bloom's favor, A retorted, that he takes his wife breakfast in bed. An ideal husband . . .

Take and give, said C. His turn will come the following morning, as we see at the start of the final episode.

In fact, having the courage to ask his wife to serve him breakfast in bed is one of Bloom's triumphs in his marital odyssey.

He may be master on the morrow, said A, but for now he serves as servant to his beloved. Her faithful follower . . .

"Hurry up with that tea," C reminded us. "Scald the teapot."

Molly orders him around, said Professor Jones, just like Mulligan did Stephen. There are many similarities between Stephen and Leopold Bloom, and both are projections of, respectively, the young Joyce and the mature man. Both are servants, dispossessed masters.

Bloom serves two mistresses, said B. Molly and the cat.

The cat mewing *Mkgnao* in the kitchen while Bloom is making the breakfast introduces us to the animal, sensual world of Molly, said C. Her first utterance is even briefer than the cat's.

Mn, said B, the first and last letters of her name, Marion.

The first word she says is a negative, said C. And the last in the last chapter is an affirmative.

In the warm saffron twilight of the bedroom, we saw the secondhand bed brought all the way from Gibraltar, and tried to imagine the way the loose quoits jingled, the *Bath of the Nymph* over the bed, the striped petticoat on the chair and the soiled drawers cast off on a corner of the bed, the open book on the floor against the one-handled orange-keyed chamber pot, while the Cicerone described Bloom's first steps outside the house, leaving the kitchen and out into the street, turning down Dorset Street until he reaches Dlugacz's butcher shop almost on the corner with Blessington Street, where he buys a kidney, returns home, picks up the letters, takes his wife her breakfast—among other imponderables, they talk about *metempsychosis* (or, as Molly says, "met him pike hoses")—then he rushes down to the kitchen again, reads a letter from his daughter Milly while he has his own breakfast, goes out to the privy at the bottom of the garden to relieve himself, reads a story in *Titbits* by somebody called Beaufoy (another name that reeks of foie gras, said A), wipes himself with a bit of the story, and when the bells of the nearby church of St. George strike a quarter to nine, tries to remember what time his friend Dignam's funeral is.

Passageways

I

Mkgnao!

The cat has just mewed, and Leopold Bloom, by the fire, is about to give her some milk in a saucer, said the Cicerone. Mr. Bloom, hands on knees, looks kindly down at the "lithe black form" and stiff tail.

He observes and is observed, said C. Bloom immediately asks himself how he must look to the cat. Like a tower?

Mrkgnao!

He tries to see things from a different point of view, even that of a cat, A said. This "relativism" is one of Bloom's good qualities.

Yes, and he does not adopt any anthropocentric attitudes towards his cat, or regard her with any false sentimentality, said C. He accepts her instincts. He knows that by nature she is cruel . . .

Mrkrgnao! B mewed again, Joyce even knew the language of cats. See how well he captured the sounds they make, for example the guttural purr as she runs to lap up the milk: *Gurrhr!*

II

A hat not simply to cover his head, said the Cicerone. He takes it from its peg.

The make of Bloom's bowler hat sounds Greek to me. *Plasto,* said Professor Jones.

And the *t* of *hat* is almost illegible from wear, B said.

Or from the sweat of his brow, cried browbeaten Professor Jones.

I am more interested in what the headband of his magician's hat is hiding, said A.

Yes, that calling card in the name of Henry Flower, said C. In the next chapter it allows him to withdraw a letter from the poste restante, sent by a woman called Martha Clifford, with whom he is maintaining a secret correspondence.

Martha must surely be another nom de plume, A said.

Martha Clifford is also the hidden Calypso of this chapter, said Professor Jones.

We will likewise see, at a crucial point in the coming night, how Dr. Bloom doffs his hat to a guard and is on the point of losing his original identity as Virag or Flower, said the Cicerone.

Virago? asked A.

III

Leopold Bloom in smartest black to show his respect at Dignam's funeral crosses over to the sunny side of the street, happily immersing himself in the warm June day that immediately transports him, as the Cicerone reminded us, to an atavistic, cliché-ridden Orient: bazaars, shuttered windows, turbaned faces . . .

The Orient of desires, said A in French. Our knight is *mal armé* for this pleasure-cruise.

The cloud he sees by St. George's steeple is the same one Stephen is contemplating in his ivory tower, said the Cicerone. It will cover the sun when Bloom comes back from buying his kidney.

IV

The Cicerone went on:

The pork butcher's, Dlugacz, is one of the few invented locations in *Ulysses*. It's another of Joyce's private jokes, referring to Moses Dlugacz (1884–1943), a Zionist rabbi who was one of Joyce's English pupils in Trieste.

Perhaps the name Moses triggered Bloom's daydreams about the Promised Land, said Professor Jones. These start when he reads about a model farm "on the lakeshore of Tiberias" on a flier he picks up in Dlugacz's shop.

What's most striking here, said C, is that Dlugacz is a pork butcher. Pig meat.

And it's a pig's kidney that Bloom buys, said B. The last one. Luckily for him, his neighbor Mr. Woods's maid does not buy it.

We ought to add in passing, A said, that the maid's "hams" also whet his appetite.

V

When he returns from buying the kidney that cost him threepence, the Cicerone observed, from the hall floor Bloom picks up a card from Milly to Molly, a letter from Milly for him, and a letter that takes him aback. It's addressed to Mrs. Marion Bloom, and is written in a bold hand. He has no need to ask who it is from, although he does just that a little later. Oh, it's from Boylan, Molly tells him in bed. Boylan is her manager and that afternoon he is going to bring her the program she is to sing at her next concert.

Here we go with the manager *à trois*, A said. And Poldy's chat with Molly is interrupted by the smell of burning. Perhaps Bloom's horns are aflame?

The kidney! B remembered. Bloom starts down the stairs like a startled stag.

The pisiform shape of that gland reminds me of something . . . said Professor Jones.

The kidney is the organ of this episode, the Cicerone reminded us, and the "New Bloomusalem" Bloom sets out to build will take the form of a huge pig's kidney.

VI

We always see Molly in bed, said the Cicerone. A bed Bloom thought Molly's father, Commander Tweedy, bought at the auction of furniture belonging to Lord Napier, the Governor of Gibraltar, although it may well be that this rank of commander was as fake as the bed—he was probably only a sergeant, but we could already hear the jingling of the quoits, the *leitmotiv* or *lit-motiv* of the adulterous bed in *Ulysses*, as B read to us that Molly has just raised herself on one elbow on the pillow: "He looked calmly down on her bulk and between her large soft bubs, sloping within her nightdress like a shegoat's udder."

Ubre de Cabra, A murmured, possibly lost in speculation about towns forever twinned in Andalucía and Ireland. Or perhaps he just said: Abracadabra.

Molly Bloom will be thirty-four on September 8, said the Cicerone. She is a dark Spanish beauty, born in Gibraltar of an Irish father—the aforementioned Commander Tweedy—and the Spanish Jew Lunita Laredo. Perhaps it was from her mother that she got her black hair and dark eyes. Despite her *bulk* (she is quite enormous, with an ample bosom, and weighs more than seventy kilos) she is very attractive and seductive.

What we first notice are her full lips and her smile as she drinks her tea. Then her mocking eyes.

"The same young eyes," according to her seduced spouse, said B.

VII

The artist's retreat, announced the Cicerone. The place where he evokes or evacuates his literary and pictorial sketches.

Holy shit! exclaimed our American Professor Jones.

Here we see Bloom the Constipated on his throne . . . A said.

Cacatio matutina, preferred or prescribed Professor Jones, *est tamquam medicina.*

All the bodily functions are presented quite naturally in *Ulysses,* C said. People urinate and defecate just as they do in real life. This upset some sensitive souls, such as Virginia Woolf, and led many to talk of Joyce's "cloacal obsession," according to an observation made by H. G. Wells that is repeated in *Ulysses* itself.

It's true, said A, that in *Ulysses* people shit and piss quite freely, and one or more of the characters even masturbates unperturbed. And yet there's no fucking in its pages.

Only words make love on the page, said B with a knowing wink.

5. THE LOTUS-EATERS

As we entered the tobacco-colored room, enveloped in the aromatic cloud from the pipe the old man with long white locks was puffing on, we glanced at and commented in passing on the information from chapter 5 of this second part that the man with the Macintosh was offering on his screen, taking a deep breath of the sweet-smelling aroma as he did so:

```
● ○ ○                        ⬜ ULYSSES II.5.doc

TITLE: The Lotus-eaters (It is also possible that the lotus flower that Ulysses' companions ate was some
kind of opiate, Professor Jones suggested . . . )

TIME: 9:40–10:15 A.M. (Bloom has traveled a mile and a quarter from his house, heading in a southwesterly
direction, said the Cicerone, and on his way he has bought a copy of the Freeman newspaper.)
```

SCIENCE, ART: Botany, chemistry (The flora in Mr. Flower's kingdom is luxuriant, said B, and so are the mysteries of the chemistry of the word.')

SYMBOL: The Eucharist (The union or family reunion, added A, as Bloom sees it. And it is significant that Joyce baptizes what in reality is St. Andrew's church as All Hallows.)

COLOR: Brown (In Joyce's final plan for the book, said C, this chapter has no color.)

TECHNIQUE: Narcissistic: narration, dialogue, interior monologue (There is a marvelous moment in which the text blooms with all the flowery tributes of Henry Flower, said C, or the "panaroma of all flores of speech," as *Finnegans Wake* has it.)

MEANING: The seduction of faith (Of all faiths, said Professor Jones, and I will close this parenthesis with a footnote.**)

CORRESPONDENCES: Lotus-eaters: Bloom (who is both a lotus-eater and Ulysses observing the dullness of his fellow citizens, said Professor Jones), several Dubliners (This chapter presents an array of characters from *Dubliners*, said the Cicerone—for example: Tom Kernan, Holohan, Bob Doran, and Martin Cunningham, while M'Coy and Bantam Lyons also make their reappearance.), carriage horses, communicants . . .

This is my body, said A, to commune with Bloom's wheel of fortune or vicious circle.

Almost immediately we saw the first stage of Bloom's itinerary displayed on the screen. From Sir John Rogerson's quay on the south bank of the Liffey, near its mouth, he strolls along until he

---

*   Chemystery, Professor Jones noted in his book.

**   Religion in general as the opiate of the people. In this chapter's odyssey, Bloom refers to the Jewish religion (Bethel, or "House of El"—"God" in Hebrew—a Salvation Army hostel on Lombard Street), to Protestantism, Buddhism, and Islam as well when he refers to Muhammad's kindness toward animals, similar to that of Bloom himself, and when he calls the bathhouse a "mosque." Bloom looks on the seduction of faith indulgently—as he does on all seductions. He is not intolerant like Stephen. But religion is not the only opiate of the people. There's also alcohol, sex, gambling, advertising . . . (Here we could spin the wheel of sports that Bloom traces at the end of this chapter, A said.)

turns south along Lime Street (It's here we meet the first lotus-eater, said B. He's the *boy for the skins*, the young rubbish collector who's smoking a cigarette butt . . .), then on down Hanover Street to the southwest, crossing Townsend Street, then further south still along the left-hand pavement of Lombard Street until he comes to Westland Row (The East in the lands of the West, said A . . . or was that Wasteland? Bloom comes to a halt in front of the Belfast and Oriental Tea Company, at Number 6), where he goes into the post office to pick up a letter sent to his alias Henry Flower by the mysterious Martha Clifford. This is Bloom's first real trip out, his first walk through the streets of Dublin, the Cicerone said, and it is noteworthy that Bloom's sauntering (He has to kill time until Dignam's funeral, said B) from the docks to the post office in Westland Row (Henry Flower in search of his flower, said A) forms a huge question mark:

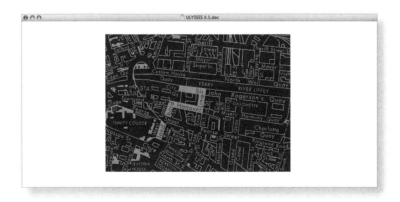

Who in fact is Martha Clifford? asked B, addressing the tigerish cat posed like a Sphinx in the doorway.

We will have to wait for her to appear in the "Circe" episode, said the Cicerone, before we are told what is possibly her real name.

Martha Clifford is also the literary transposition of Marthe Fleischmann, said Professor Jones. The woman Joyce had a secret epistolary romance with in Zurich from December, 1918 to March, 1919.

For precision's sake, said the Cicerone, we should note that in his correspondence with Marthe Fleischmann, Joyce wrote the two *E*s of his name as Greek epsilons, just like Henry Flower did.

What is the yellow flower Martha sends Henry Flower in her letter? A wondered. A narcissus would be appropriate. Apart from the rather obvious rebus, it is curious she should ask him what kind of perfume his wife wears. Amour in a Moorish scent?

Useful for him to find the pin at this point, Professor Jones said. For now we can leave his reply or the perfume floating in midair . . .

The panacea, said A. Odors against ardors . . .

Popular perfume or pop . . . the Cicerone started to explain.

In this episode Bloom the lotus-eater is intoxicated by his odorless flower, said Professor Jones. And by his own hair oil, and even by the smell of the newsprint (the most powerful drug?) from his newspaper.

He's a *Freeman* to smell as he pleases, A said.

Or to read Martha's letter on the sly, said B.

Or to *Throwaway* the letter, C said.

A fantastic episode, the Cicerone explained. When Bloom offers Bantam Lyons his paper, telling him he was thinking of throwing it away, Bantam thinks Bloom's giving him a tip for the Gold Cup being run at Ascot that same day. And as we see from the *Evening Telegraph* later on, *Throwaway* was indeed the winning horse.

But for now Bloom's attention and compassion are for another kind of horse, Professor Jones said. The ones he sees as he passes the cabman's shelter.

"Poor jugginses," B recalled, "with their long noses stuck in nosebags."

Although Bloom also thinks they might be happy to be castrated, when he sees the "stump of black guttapercha wagging limp between their haunches."

After taking in the smell of horse urine and his almost odorless flower, the perfume-expert Professor Jones informed us, Bloom goes into All Hallows church by the back door, drawn by the "cold smell of sacred stone."

His senses reel with the smell of incense, said A. And the melted candle wax . . .

But he remains sufficiently alert to follow the ceremony, said B, and to realize at the end of Mass that he's left the bottom two buttons on his waistcoat undone.

He also notices the priest's sole peeping out from among the lace of his cassock when he knelt down.

From the church Bloom goes to Sweny's pharmacy on Lincoln Place. It's still there today, said the Cicerone, because as Bloom himself says, "Chemists rarely move." After smelling different potions, he orders a lotion for Molly (which our "lotus-eater" forgets to pick up), buys a cake of soap ("Sweet lemony wax," B quoted—Barrington soap, for fourpence) which plays an important role throughout *Ulysses*. (Like the potato-talisman Bloom always carries with him, said C. He inherited it from his mother.) He is still clutching it when he heads for the "mosque" of the Turkish baths on Leinster Street.

The baths are no longer there, but used to stand opposite Finn's Hotel, where the young Nora Barnacle worked as a maid on that June 16, 1904.

But Bloom did not know that, said C sarcastically. He heads for the baths with masturbatory intentions, intending to read the letter.

Missive impossible, said A. Bloom has no intention of going beyond words to deeds and ever clinching with Clifford.

He has no need to meet her in person, said B. Love letters are far safer.

It was for literary purposes that Bloom first got in touch, C said. He put an ad in the paper.

In the *Irish Times*, B recalled. "Wanted, smart lady typist to aid gentleman in literary work."

Bloom sticks to his role, said A. He does not want to pass to the "other world," the other side of the paper . . .

He prefers the world of words, B said.

C said, That mistake made by the secretary Martha Clifford: putting *world* instead of *word*—"I do not like that other world"— is another theme in *Ulysses* and another link between Bloom and Stephen, because in "Circe," the latter's mother appears, telling him she has come from the other world.

There is still a long way to go from the stems of "The Lotus-eaters" to the storms of "Circe," A pointed out.

It is fitting that the lotus-eaters episode ends not with a real bath, but the daydream of a bath, C said.

Almost worthy of Archimedes, said A. Bloom's discovery could be baptized his Eucharistic Eureka.

Passageways

I

Bloom stares at the window of the Belfast and Oriental Tea Company, A said. All those neatly labeled packets that anesthetize his mind with ethereal promises of a tawdry Orient, a *dolce far niente.*

Brilliant smells and colors . . . said B, slowly passing her right hand over her brow and hair.

Local synesthesia, A said with a smile, for all the senses.

Belfast is the last stop on Molly's tour with her manager Boylan, B reminded us.

Bloom's wooing in front of the window will be with another woman, said A. He's just taken the card with his flowery pseudonym out of his hatband, and put it in his waistcoat pocket.

I would concentrate on the shape of the tea-packet labels, said C.

They are all circular, said Professor Jones. Don't forget, the Eucharist is the symbol of this chapter.

II

From looking at the tea shop window, said the Cicerone, Bloom's mind wanders through Edenic daydreams, and then to a photograph of a man in the Dead Sea reading flat on his back because the water's so salty. Bloom starts to drown in a sea of doubt as he tries to remember the Archimedes Principle.

The Dead Sea became a graveyard, A said.

III

While Bloom is trying to hurry up so that he can read Martha Clifford's letter in private, said the Cicerone, and is enjoying the other solitary pleasure that is voyeurism—he has just caught sight of an elegant lady about to get into a carriage outside the door of the Grosvenor Hotel—the tiresome M'Coy steps into his path and his visual field.

M'Coy is trying to tell him the story about valises that he uses to snare the unwary, said A.

Yes, said the Cicerone, he asks to borrow valises for his wife's supposed tours. She is also a professional soprano, like Molly.

Molly is much better, said B. That's what Bloom proudly thinks. Although Molly hasn't sung for a year.

Look! said A. Look at what the Peeping Bloom Tom is missing.

"High brown boots with laces dangling," recalled B. "Well-turned foot."

Peeping! A insisted.

"Rich: silk stockings," said B.

A clanging tram prevents him seeing any more, said the Cicerone. Bloom recalls the image of a girl fixing her garter in a doorway in Eustace Street (which we will come across again in the "Wandering Rocks" chapter) while a girlfriend covered her.

Garde du corps, said A.

IV

Shut your eyes and open your mouth, A said.

With hat and head tilted backward . . . said the Cicerone.

Stick the tongue out, said A.

. . . and he puts it neatly into the mouth, the Cicerone went on, of each of the women kneeling to take communion before the altar rail in All Hallows church. The priest goes along handing out the host and murmuring in Latin.

Latin to stupefy, thinks Bloom, said C.

And communion as an opiate, A said.

Bloom studies the ritual of communion with the objectivity of an ethnologist, said C. He goes beyond the form to the mysterious depths of theophagy. Behind communion, in his view, there is a transcendent idea, and a trance—the feeling of carrying the kingdom of God inside oneself.

V

At the pharmacy, Bloom orders the lotion for Molly. It made her skin a delicate white and brought out the darkness of her eyes, said the Cicerone. Bloom remembers her looking at him with the sheet drawn up to her eyes, *Spanish*, looking at him and smelling herself while he put on his cufflinks.

And while he goes on "perfumemorying," said A, he remembers the question about the perfume his wife uses that his secret correspondent asked him, and adds as an afterthought, *Peau d'Espagne*.

So long as it's not *peau pourrie* . . . B said.

The skin is the part of the body to which this chapter is dedicated, C said.

Above all, the finest, most delicate skin, said A, raising her eyebrows.

Molly's skin or moleskin? asked B.

VI

After leaving Bantam Lyons with his ridiculous tip on the winning horse, Bloom turns onto Lincoln Place, then walks cheerfully down Leinster Street towards the bathhouse, situated at Number 11. Its red bricks and minarets make him think of a mosque.

Mental marquetry, said C, of a fantasy Orient.

Rouge montage, said A. Red-baked brick-à-brac.

VII

"This is my body," Bloom thinks, imagining himself in the bath, the Cicerone explained.

The corolla and chalice, A repeated his corollary: A new transubstantiation of Mr. Flower floating in the water.

"Father of thousands," "a languid floating flower," B quoted.

Undoubtedly an allusion to the flower of the *Saxifraga stolonifera* plant, said Professor Jones, known as the "mother of thousands" because of its many seeds. Or perhaps I mean the *Saxifraga sarmentosa*.

I prefer to think of a sexier flower, A said. An orchid, for example . . .

6. HADES

A really long funeral march . . . said A, when he heard the Cicerone explain that Patrick Dignam's cortege crosses the whole of Dublin, from southeast to northwest (about four miles altogether) accompanying the deceased from his house at 9 Newbridge Avenue in the coastal suburb of Sandymount to his final resting place in Glasnevin Cemetery where, among other renowned Irishmen, lies the body of the nationalist leader Charles Stewart Parnell (1846–1891), the man who inspired Joyce's first poem, "Et tu, Healy," written at the age of nine.

It is also the resting place of another Irish hero, said C: Daniel O'Connell (1775–1847), known as the Liberator, whose heart remained in Rome.

In order not to lose perspective, said A, we should remember the cemetery is officially called "Prospect" . . .

"Paltry funeral," Bloom says to himself. The cortege, with the hearse and three mourning carriages, crosses the four rivers of Hades in Dublin, in this order: the Dodder, the Grand Canal, the Liffey, and the Royal Canal, said the Cicerone. They are burying Dignam-Elpenor, who died of a heart attack brought on by his fondness for drink.

⚫◯◯	ULYSSES II.6.doc	

TITLE: Hades	TECHNIQUE: Incubism—narration, dialogue, interior monologue
SETTING: Cemetery	
	MEANING: Descent into nothingness
TIME: 11:00–11:45 A.M.	
	CORRESPONDENCES:
SYMBOL: Cemetery, Sacred Heart,	Sisyphus: Cunningham
the Unknown Stranger	Cerberus: Father Coffey
	Hades: John O'Connell
COLOR: Black, white	Hercules: Daniel O'Connell
	Elpenor: Dignam
ORGAN: Heart	Agamemnon: Parnell

One of Bloom's traveling companions, the bearded, silk-hatted Martin Cunningham also has a problem with drink, said A. His wife's drinking problem, that is. She drinks all the housekeeping money and every Saturday pawns the furniture. On Mondays she starts all over again . . .

"And they call me the jewel of Asia," B hummed. She dances in a drunken state clutching her husband's umbrella.

Patient Martin Cunningham, whose intelligent face reminds Bloom of Shakespeare's, C said, knows a lot about drunks . . .

In this chapter too we meet again several of the characters from *Dubliners*, said the Cicerone. In the horse-drawn carriage where

Bloom is traveling (A rather ramshackle, dirty affair, B commented, with bread crumbs on its mildewed leather seat . . .) there are two characters from "Grace": the aforementioned Martin Cunningham and Jack Power, the youngest of the group. In the earlier story they were trying to rehabilitate the drunkard Tom Kernan. And here is Simon Dedalus too, Stephen's father, from the *Portrait* . . .

A portrait from life, of John Joyce, James's father, A said. Though not a model father . . .

Joyce portrays him masterfully in the *Portrait*, C said. A spendthrift, a drinker, a good storyteller . . .

Simon Dedalus had tried to flirt with Molly in the past, B said.

In the "Ithaca" episode, Bloom includes Simon in the fantastic list of Molly's lovers, C said. When he sees his angry face opposite him in the carriage, he remembers Molly looking out of her window at a pair of mongrel dogs mating.

She was in mating mood too, said A. Almost at once she became pregnant with Rudy.

The dead child . . . B said. And Simon Dedalus's wife is in Glasnevin Cemetery too.

The heart, the organ that dominates this chapter, Professor Jones explained, is both the machine that stops at the end of life and the symbolic seat of the emotions: the heart broken by grief and sadness when it recalls those who have gone to the other world.

Let us look, the Cicerone said, at the position of the travelers in the carriage: in the back seats are Leopold Bloom (the only one not silk-hatted, wearing his eternal bowler) with, on his right, Jack Power; opposite them, with their backs to the coachman, sit Simon Dedalus, and, on his left, the bearded Martin Cunningham.

On College Street we pass the strange fountain-plant (*Trepical*, A said, or *delirical* . . .), foliage in memory of Sir Philip Crampton (1777–1858). Who could that be? Bloom wonders. A Dublin surgeon, but his monument disappeared long ago.

Another more upsetting vision soon startles Bloom: the person who that same afternoon is to become his wife's lover (Bloom never says his name: Blazes Boylan), dashing and elegant, outside the Red Bank restaurant and oyster bar (Her manager, A said, who is going to manage to manhandle Molly . . .). Two episodes later, while he's eating in Davy Byrne's pub, Bloom will recall this fleeting glimpse of Boylan in the restaurant doorway, and will not forget that oysters are an aphrodisiac . . .

The conversation in the carriage is sometimes serious and sometimes becomes rather comic, as when the passengers tell the story of a frustrated suicide who was "fished" out of the Liffey, although when they delve deeper into the topic of suicide and its condemnation on moral and Christian grounds, sympathetic Cunningham tries to change the subject.

One of the shades from the other world that returns to haunt Bloom is that of his father Rudolph Bloom, who on June 27, 1886, committed suicide by taking poison (aconite) at the Queen's Hotel in Ennis, which he owned. Bloom sees in his mind the hotel bedroom with its hunting prints, the bottle with its red label on the bedside table, the dead body at the foot of the bed.

Bloom's emotional nature, his true humanity and sensibility, do not prevent him having a practical side, a materialist concept of life.

After watching, not without irony, the religious service in the chapel, led by Father Coffey (whose name reminds him of the word *coffin*) and then respectfully following Dignam's coffin to the grave (on the way he sadly sees the pathetic spectacle of Simon Dedalus crying over his wife, who is buried close by), Bloom reflects on life and resurrection. Once you are dead, you are dead, he concludes with crushing, if trite, logic. When he remembers the phrase Jack Power spoke to Dedalus—"How many broken hearts are buried here, Simon!"—his inventor's mind leads him to think: "old rusty pumps." In fact, on the way to the cemetery, Bloom has had several practical ideas, including a tramline to take cattle to the quays; he also thinks it would be a good idea to set up a line of funeral trams, and in the cemetery it occurs to him that they could have a gramophone in every grave.

His Master's Voice! A exclaimed. All that's missing is the fox terrier *Nipper* . . .

Athos rather, C said. Bloom's father's dog.

Let's listen again to that wonderful voice of the Master, B said. "*Kraahraark! Hellohellohello amawfullyglad kraark awfullygladaseeagain hellohello amawf krpthsth.*"

The voice raising the dead from beyond the grave, A said.

The inventor Leopold Bloom is the son of Bouvard and Pécuchet, said C.

Behind Dignam's coffin he might have shouted: And to think we dined together only a week ago! . . . Who would have thought it!

At any rate, Bloom does not "like that other world" either, said C. He is relieved to get out of the cemetery.

"Back to the world again," B quoted. "Enough of this place."

Passageways

I

Also in mourning . . . Ineluctable modality of the visible, A exclaimed. Son ahoy!

Yes, in Irishtown, beyond Watery Lane (nowadays called Dermot O'Hurley Avenue), said B. From the carriage Bloom sees a lithe young man dressed in mourning wearing a broad-brimmed hat.

Bought in the Latin Quarter, A specified. Our closet Hamlet has just been strolling on Sandymount beach.

This is the first time the paths of the main characters in *Ulysses* cross, C said. From now on they will come ever nearer.

So near and yet so far, A said.

"There's a friend of yours gone by," Bloom tells Simon Dedalus, said the Cicerone. Dedalus asks him who it was.

"Your son and heir," Bloom replies, though he doesn't really know Stephen himself, yet, said B.

Still, the absence of a son since Rudy's death is soon occupying his thoughts, said C.

An unknown man is observing them all, B said, worried.

A specter in perspective. In Prospect, said A.

The Cicerone went on: In the doorway of the Red Bank on D'Olier Street, they see the flash of a straw boater. "Worst man in Dublin," or so Bloom thinks.

Blazes Boylan is also based on Gogarty, A said. He gets everywhere: he is the playful Mulligan and the Playboy Boylan.

II

Black, white, black . . .

A tragic case . . .

From his carriage Bloom observes how on the corner of Sackville (now O'Connell) Street and Cavendish Road (now Parnell Street), a white coffin in a black hearse pulled by white horses with white plumes goes by in a flash, said the Cicerone. He pointed his wand at the corner of the Rotunda (that group of eighteenth-century public buildings).

Little angels on their way to heaven, A said. (Or did he say haven?)

It really does go by in a flash, C said. In Glasnevin Cemetery, Bloom wonders what has become of the white coffin.

III

As the mourning carriage passes not far from Eccles Street ("My house down there," says Bloom), they are surrounded by a herd of cattle . . .

Calves and scarves, A interrupted the Cicerone: a labyrinth to lose your rag in.

And in the midst of the cattle, said the Cicerone, "ran raddled sheep bleating their fear."

Perhaps they sense, B said, that "tomorrow is killing day."

IV

B said:

The mysterious stranger in the brown macintosh. "Now who is he I'd like to know?"

The man in the macintosh, A said. Or simply M'Intosh by name, as reported in the obituaries section of the *Evening Telegraph*.

Who is the man in the macintosh? C wondered. That is one of the mysteries of *Ulysses*. Bloom wonders who he is at the end of his odyssey.

Perhaps Joyce took the secret with him to his grave, B said.

Professor Nabokov and many others think it's Joyce himself appearing in his work like Hitchcock did in his films, A said. The author dropping in unannounced.

When he realizes the stranger makes thirteen at Dignam's funeral, B said, Bloom thinks the man may be Death.

The man in the macintosh is really "the invisible man," said C. All we see of him is his raincoat. And it is fitting that his first appearance and disappearance come in the "Hades" episode, because in Greek, *Hades* means "the invisible."

The man in the macintosh also wears the "cloak of invisibility," A said.

We have to correct our own man with the Macintosh, said Professor Jones, turning to the impassive lanky figure, because in his *Correspondences*, it doesn't mention that the man in the macintosh is Hades . . .

Was Hades the man in the macintosh? A asked.

Was *Noman* the shadow of a shadow in Hades? asked C.

So who was the man in the macintosh? B asked.

A huge question mark glowed black on the Macintosh screen.

V

After visiting Parnell's grave with his companions (Power tells them that some people believe there are only stones in the tomb, and that the "chief" will return one day), Bloom makes his way past sad angels, crosses, broken columns, family vaults, stone hopes, the hands and hearts of old Ireland, the Cicerone said. Pomp and circumstance bursting like bubbles. The remains of so many renowned names. Bloom's practical turn of mind thinks it would be more sensible to use all the money spent on stones as charity for the living.

VI

Moldy crowns, rusty tin wreaths, the Cicerone went on, the Sacred Heart with his heart in his hand. Bloom thinks it should be painted red like a real heart.

What really attracts Bloom's attention and awakens his vivid emotional response to life, C said, is a bird sitting on a poplar branch.

As if stuffed, said B. It reminds him of when his daughter Milly buried a dead bird in a box of kitchen matches.

7. AEOLUS

IN THE LUNGS OF THE HIBERNIAN METROPOLIS

In its caverns . . . A said.

The realms of Aeolus and of the *Freeman* and *Evening Telegraph* newspapers, said the Cicerone. At that time they were in the same building, on Prince Street, near the column of the "onehandled adulterer" (the blind man of Trafalgar, A said), from which the two old women launch their plum pits, or "aeroliths," in the chapter's final parable.

Before we come to the newspapers and their headlines, and shoot through the printing room, *Sllt*, for a moment we hear the thud of the beer barrels (The fuel that sets off the Dubliners' gossip-mongering and loosens their tongues, A commented), which roll along the cul de sac in the center of the city, and resound again.

Repetition for effect, A said.

Sometimes the rhetorical effects of "Aeolus" come in pairs, like lungs: in, said Professor Jones—snorting as he did so—and out.

Another "barreltone," A said. The rhetorical jousting in this chapter ought to figure in the Guinness Book of Records.

If the cemetery was the heart of Dublin ("The Irishman's house is his coffin," thought Bloom), the lungs of the city are in "Aeolus," Professor Jones went on: the *Freeman* and the *Telegraph*, which Bloom and Stephen visit around noon (their paths cross again, although the time for them to meet has not yet come). The former is trying to place an ad, the latter to see if they will publish Mr. Deasy's foot-and-mouth letter.

SHORT BUT TO THE POINT

And boy is it to the point! A exclaimed, staring at the man with the Macintosh

	ULYSSES II.7.doc	
TITLE: Aeolus	ORGAN: Lungs
SETTING: The newspaper	TECHNIQUE: Enthymemes
TIME: 12:00–1:00 P.M.	MEANING: The ridiculousness of victory
SCIENCE, ART: Rhetoric	CORRESPONDENCES:
	Aeolus: Crawford
SYMBOL: Machinery, wind, kite, printing press, editor	Aeolus's floating island: the newspaper
COLOR: Red	

Enti . . . ? said B, frowning.

Yes, entimematics, C explained. The technique of *entimema*, enthymeme, the shortened form of a syllogism in which one of the propositions is understood (I dispute the major premise, said A, shaking his head), or when an argument is reduced to a single sentence. This is very much to the point for newspaper articles and headlines. Or for rhetorical effect in a speech. Aristotle, Joyce's favorite philosopher, called the enthymeme the orator's syllogism.

This chapter, which features the easy talk of Dubliners as well as the eloquence of some Dublin lawyers like Seymour Bushe and the tribune John F. Taylor, is dedicated to rhetoric and oratory.

Joyce chose Taylor's speech in favor of Irish language and culture for the only sound recording ever made of him reading *Ulysses*.

Gone with the wind . . . A snorted. Words fly; they are what put the air in Eire.

Where? B asked.

Enthymeme, concluded A.

THE NUMBERS GAME

Speaking of words, B said, how many are there in *Ulysses*?

The Macintosh screen immediately showed these words and figures:

```
                    Ulysses

        Total number of words: 260,430
        Total number of unique words: 29,899
```

Are you sure? C asked, turning to the man with the Macintosh. I think those figures are out of date.

GONE WITH THE WIND. TARA!

C said:

After hearing secondhand or second mouth the *morceaux de bravoure* of a speech by Taylor in favor of Irish nationalism, C said, Stephen mentally defines oratorical hyperbole as what is gone with the wind.

And then he immediately mentions Tara! B exclaimed.

Tara, said C, the seat of the ancient kings of Ireland.

A different Tara, said A.

Can Margaret Mitchell have read *Ulysses*? B asked.

A useful topic for a galloping assumption; A clicked his tongue and added, This is turning more scarlet than red.

RHYMES AND REASONS

But Stephen has had enough of all this overblown rhetoric, said B. "Dead noise," he calls it, and proposes that "the house do now adjourn."

And invites his companions to the pub, C said.

To Mooney's, said B, even though this means he is standing up Mulligan and Haines, who are expecting to see him at half past twelve not far away in another pub, the Ship.

Stephen also contrasts the ephemeral nature of oratory and journalism to the permanence of poetry, C said.

And the rather poor verses he wrote on a piece of Mr. Deasy's letter will resound like kisses . . . said A.

There is no room for poetry in the newspaper, C said. After he has given Deasy's letter to Crawford, the editor urges him to write something "with a bite in it."

"DO-IT-YOURSELF!"

Stephen is as out of place in the newspaper office as Bloom is, said B.

Crawford has no better suggestion for Stephen than a satirical local color piece, C said, in which "all Dublin" will figure: "Put us all into it," he tells him.

YOU CAN DO IT! is the title of that column in the newspaper, B said. And in *Ulysses*, Joyce showed in no uncertain terms that he could.

Years later, once he had properly studied his portable Dublin, A said. As Stephen tells himself in a rare moment of modesty: "Dublin. I have much, much to learn."

Stephen and Bloom cross in the street for an instant, C said. Bloom notes as he passes by that Stephen is wearing a good pair of boots today.

The kid-leather boots, A said. The ones belonging to the "Buck" . . .

Let's retrace our steps, C proposed, or rather Bloom's, and follow the Cicerone.

AN AD CANVASSER CANVASSED . . .

The Cicerone said:

Just as in the second chapter we saw Stephen teaching in Mr. Deasy's school, in this one we see Leopold Bloom at work trying to place an ad for his client Alexander Keyes: a tea, wine, and spirits merchant. He tries to get it into the *Evening Telegraph*, whose editor Myles Crawford—as Aeolus does with Ulysses—at first receives him warmly but in the end dismisses him out of hand: "Tell him go to hell . . ."

In this "Aeolus" there are countless references to the wind, C said.

Someone even plays a peculiar "aeolian harp," said B, with a thread between their teeth. *Bingbang, bangbang.*

C went on:

Gusts of wind blow, doors slam, papers fly through the air, there are draughts everywhere . . .

And in the end Bloom is truly deflated, A said.

SERIOUS REVERSAL

The Cicerone continued:

After visiting the office of the foreman Joseph Nannetti, who is more concerned with a letter from the archbishop than the adjustments to Alexander Keyes's ad, Bloom goes through the case room where there's an old man wearing glasses and an apron, the *dayfather* Monks (who has dedicated his entire life—a modest, honest one—to his profession); Bloom stops then to watch how a typesetter is composing the name *mangiD kcirtaP*. This reminds him of poor Rudolph Bloom, R.I.P., reading in Hebrew and moving his finger from right to left.

If he had carried on watching the typesetter setting the article on Dignam's funeral, B said, he would have noticed the mistake that changed his name to Boom.

Yes, Leopold Boom, C said. Missing the *L* that Martha put one too many of in her letter. But to see this new erratum, he will have to wait until the antepenultimate chapter.

"Eumaeus," said A.

THE TAIL OF THE KITE

In the *Evening Telegraph* offices, explained the Cicerone, Bloom witnesses several oratorical jousts. Those taking part include the Latin professor MacHugh, and two of his companions at Dignam's funeral, Simon Dedalus and Ned Lambert.

As in the previous chapter, Bloom is sometimes treated condescendingly, at others he is ignored, or even dismissed rudely. Or he remains on the margins, not getting involved in the jokes or double entendres that he is not interested in or which he does not understand. A foreigner in his own country.

There is something of Chaplin about Bloom too, said B. People make fun of him or ridicule him. Take the scene where Bloom leaves the newspaper offices to go to find Alexander Keyes, and

from the window Professor MacHugh and the sports reporter
Lenehan are amused at the way "the file of capering newsboys"
follow behind Bloom. One of them is carrying a kite with a tail,
and follows him imitating his flat-footed way of walking.

FAILING LIST

In addition to being a catalogue of rhetorical figures, Professor Jones said, this chapter is also a catalogue of failures. Joyce
indicated that the "meaning" of "Aeolus" was "The Derision of
Victory." Pyrrhus, Moses, and several Irish revolutionaries are
mentioned again, and a number of correspondences are drawn
between the peoples of Israel and Ireland. Moses did not reach
the Promised Land, Irish nationalism did not achieve its goal,
and on his own small scale, Bloom does not secure the promised
ad, the keys to his kingdom. In addition, almost all the characters
who appear in this chapter are failures or suffer their small daily
reverses.

Bloom also fails once more to get Hynes to pay him back the
three shillings he's owed him for three weeks already, said C.

Who? asked B.

Joe Hynes, C said. The reporter who wrote the article about
Dignam's funeral.

Passageways

I

THE QUILL BEHIND THE EAR

Here is Red Murray, the Cicerone said, with his long shears . . .

Red is a fitting name, said A. This chapter's color is red. And there are "reds" and "bloodies" everywhere.

In real life he was John Murray, C said. A maternal uncle of Joyce's, known as "Murray the Redhead" or Red Murray. He worked as a bookkeeper on the *Freeman*.

The door to the office creaked again, B said.

With "four clean strokes," Red Murray, pen behind his ear, cuts out the advert for Alexander Keyes which Bloom has to take to the *Evening Telegraph* printing works, said the Cicerone.

The drawing of the two crossed keys is not on the ad, C said. As yet it is only in Bloom's mind.

And in the name Keyes, said A.

The quill behind the ear, B pointed out, could be the emblem of *Ulysses* itself.

Also the scissors and paste that are mentioned after Red Murray has cut out the ad, C said. Joyce saw himself as a "scissors and paste" author.

II

A SET OF KEYS

The Cicerone explained about the ad for the dealer in tea, wines, and spirits (A good way to complete the Trinity, A said): Alexander Keyes is a verbal and visual play on the words *Keyes* and *Keys*, and also refers to the "House of Keys," or parliament on the Isle of Man.

The keys represent Irish autonomy, C said. They are also the keys of Saint Peter on the Vatican's crest. The keys to Catholic Ireland.

There are a lot of other esoteric and symbolic allusions in the keys as well, Professor Jones said. Don't forget that when he explained the drawing to the foreman Nannetti, Bloom crossed his fingers . . .

And Bloom and Stephen's paths cross again, said A, when Bloom goes to the National Library in search of a drawing of the keys in a Kilkenny paper.

We could also imagine as crossed the two keys Stephen and Bloom have left behind: the one for the Martello tower, the other for 7 Eccles Street, said C.

They themselves are key, A said. The two key characters . . .

And don't forget the master key, B said. Or better still in French, the *clef maitresse*, because Joyce called *Ulysses* his "mistresspiece," his best-loved work.

Yes, best-loved, A said, but in English it is *master* key, the key of the Master . . .

As Anna Livia Plurabelle announces at the end of *Finnegans Wake*, said C, "The keys to. Given!"

Given in parody, A said. In a masterful way.

III

PERFUMED SOAP

As Bloom raises his handkerchief to his nose, he notices the smell of the soap he bought at Sweney's pharmacy two chapters earlier, and used in his Turkish bath.

He put his handkerchief back in the top pocket of his jacket, the Cicerone said, and slipped the soap into the hip pocket of his trousers, where he kept it during the journey to the cemetery, only to move the uncomfortable lump to his handkerchief pocket when he got down from the carriage. The cake of soap appears and is smelled in almost every chapter: it is in the next one, in "The Sirens," in "Nausicaa," and returns in all its splendor in "Circe" . . .

The soap is another of Bloom's talismans, like the potato he keeps in his pocket, C said. He keeps the soap with him all the time, from the moment he takes a bath in "The Lotus-eaters" to when he washes his hands in "Ithaca."

The odyssey of Bloom's soap would make a good soap opera, A said.

But you are overlooking the essential part of the scene, said B. When Bloom smells the cake of soap as he's going down the newspaper office steps, it reminds him of Martha's question about what perfume his wife uses.

Yes, what perfume is it? A repeated.

We'll find out later, C said.

Bloom immediately thinks he could go home with the excuse he has forgotten something, said B. He could sniff his wife's perfumes and catch her still dressing.

Soap-sap! A exclaimed. Fatefully, however, he decides despite himself: *No*.

IV

AVE, CRAWFORD

What is *that*? B had said.

The cock of the walk, Myles Crawford, the editor of the *Evening Telegraph*, the Cicerone explained. Our irascible Aeolus has just come in.

During the night of grace and disgrace in the "Circe" episode, C said, he reappears with a bird's feather in his beak to caw obscenities, on a par with what he shouts at Bloom here: "He can kiss my royal Irish arse."

Crawford is graphically described earlier in the chapter. B read:

"The inner door was opened violently and a scarlet beaked face, crested by a comb of feathery hair, thrust itself in."

V

ANOTHER PUFF

The Cicerone said:

Myles Crawford violently projected the first puff of smoke up toward the ceiling.

Aeolus himself could not have done it better, A said.

Especially since the island of Aeolus is usually identified with Stromboli, said C.

VI

THE NAME OF THE ROSE OF CASTILE

The riddle that Lenehan the sports reporter proposes to his colleagues and friends at the newspaper, the Cicerone said—"What opera resembles a railway line?"—is remembered by Bloom on several occasions throughout the day of *Ulysses*.

A few paragraphs further on, in the newspaper office, Lenehan proudly tells them the answer:

"The Rose of Castile. See the wheeze? Rows of cast steel. Gee!"

Railing at the rails, A said.

Paronomasia, Professor Jones said. And this operatic *Rose of Castile* takes on a different color and odor if we bear in mind that the "Spanish" singer Madam Bloom is shortly to be mentioned, after Bloom has already left, when Lenehan (one of the two gallants in the story of the same name in *Dubliners*) makes an allusion that will become more comprehensible when we reach his conversation with M'Coy in "Wandering Rocks." There he tells him he had sung one or two duets with Molly once when they were squashed in a carriage with her husband.

Don't play it again, A said. That's the *Rose of Castile* for you.

VII

STANDING STONES

The Cicerone said:

After Stephen has heard Taylor's well-molded words about Michelangelo's *Moses*—"that stony effigy in frozen music, horned and terrible"—and the monolithic speeches about Moses in Egypt—Stephen has the mental image of "a man supple in combat: stone-horned, stonebearded, heart of stone."

And Stephen has to be supple in his fight against rhetoric, C said. Against the petrifaction of language.

To avoid being petrified himself, A said. Or being stoned, because it's no accident that he bears the name of the proto-martyr Stephen . . .

8. THE LAESTRYGONIANS

Lick your fingers and your knuckles too, because the menu is succulent, B exclaimed when the Cicerone told us that anyone with
a weak stomach should avoid tasting (or did he say *wasting*?) the
dishes on the *magna carta* Bloom offers us at lunchtime: the reverend Dr. Salmon, tinned salmon, all kinds of poached and boiled
eggs, Dignam's potted meat with lemon and rice, sweetbreads of
white missionary, of the Reverend MacTrigger, and many other
house specials that we see and are served.

Likewise Rabelaisian—for gargantuan gorges and pantagruelic
Irish hunger—is the soup kitchen Bloom dreams up, where the vat
of soup is as big as Phoenix Park.

It's fable soup, A said. Aesophagus's fable . . .

And from Bloom's overheated mind and his mythical pot, we
get, "Harpooning flitches and hindquarters out of it," which recalls

the description of the Laestrygonians spearing Ulysses' companions like fish.

The parallel with the cannibals in the *Odyssey* reaches its culmination when Bloom visits the Burton restaurant and flees in disgust at the spectacle of all the men eating there.

The Adoration of the Phagia, A said.

Yes, that's what this chapter could be called, C said, staring at the screen.

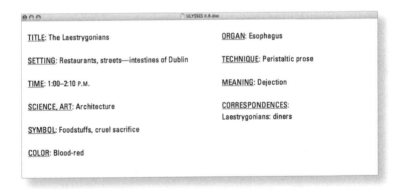

TITLE: The Laestrygonians

ORGAN: Esophagus

SETTING: Restaurants, streets—intestines of Dublin

TECHNIQUE: Peristaltic prose

TIME: 1:00–2:10 P.M.

MEANING: Dejection

SCIENCE, ART: Architecture

CORRESPONDENCES:
Laestrygonians: diners

SYMBOL: Foodstuffs, cruel sacrifice

COLOR: Blood-red

In fact, Bloom's gastronomic tour begins with dessert: "Pineapple rock, lemon platt, butter scotch," as Bloom passes by the "warm sweet fumes" of Graham Lemon's sweetshop (in reality Lemon & Co. Limited) at 49 Sackville (now O'Connell) Street, as he watches how a "sugarsticky girl" serves scoops of creams to a Christian brother. This leads him to think it must be for some school celebration, and being bighearted (and sensible) he immediately thinks: "Bad for their tummies." Almost at once a young man from the YMCA thrusts a leaflet into his hand. This announces that Elijah is coming. To begin with, Bloom gets confused with the first letters *Bloo*, thinking it might be his name, but then he realizes it is only the *Blood of the Lamb*. His mind is already dwelling on various bloody victims, and the "kidney burntoffering" he had for breakfast.

Another religious image, a luminous crucifix used in an ad, gleams in his keen mind, and he remembers the phosphorescent glow he once saw over a piece of cod in his kitchen pantry.

The mystical ichthyologic association between Christ and fish in Greek, between God and cod in English is strengthened still further if we remember that Bloom's childhood nickname was *Mackerel*.

If he carries on with the fish-cum-cross, A said, he won't leave a single bone.

It is lunchtime, and Bloom is hungry, said the Cicerone. As he walks from the *Freeman* to the National Library, he chews over his memories and whets them with images and metaphors for food. This appetite wakens other appetites (the sexual one as well). It could be said that in this chapter Bloom sees everything through the veil of his palate . . . For example, the first time he thinks of Molly here it is because of some *Malaga raisins* she had a craving for while she was pregnant with Rudy. Soon afterwards he sees with compassion how Stephen Dedalus's young sister is standing outside Dillon's auction rooms on Bachelor's Walk, doubtless selling some old bits of furniture. He says to himself that as well as being badly dressed she is undernourished, with a poor diet: "Potatoes and marge, marge and potatoes."

Heading southward, when he reaches O'Connell Bridge he sees a barge loaded with beer barrels (drink is important as well in this episode). A few minutes later this has become transformed—when he remembers and celebrates a joke by Molly—into Ben Dollard's *barreltone* (he was a bass), and a barrel of Bass . . .

For a moment on the bridge, he contemplates suicide ("If I threw myself down?") but decides instead to throw his leaflet to the seagulls (symbolically, Elijah is also Bloom, as we shall see). Joyce calls the leaflet a *throwaway* (the same name as the horse that wins the Ascot Gold Cup), and a few chapters later we will follow it as it races downstream . . .

The gulls are famished, as a "peristaltic" couplet repeated in the text tells us, but they are not fooled by the wet ball of paper, so roly-poly Bloom buys two buns for a penny from an old woman and throws them the crumbs from the bridge.

Life is a stream, Bloom tells himself in a monologue or stream of consciousness. He follows the associations brought back by some notices about venereal disease he saw once in a public urinal, until he's brought up with a jolt, what if he . . . Blazes Boylan (Bloom still does not mention him by name) . . . but after a rocky moment he succeeds in dismissing the idea, and goes on daydreaming about a happier time in the past, which, when he sees some aptly named sandwich men, each with a scarlet letter on their white hats—H, E, L, Y, S—takes him back to the time when he was newly married ("I was happier then," he tells himself more than once) and worked in Hely's stationery and printing shop on Dame Street—although it seems Bloom's brilliant advertising ideas were not appreciated there.

Wiping the slate clean, Bloom crosses Westmoreland Street and remembers happy household scenes from the past: bathing his little daughter for example, or the affectionate memories he has of a charity dinner in Glencree he went to with Molly. She was just starting to grow plump, and attracted people's glances in her tightly fitting elephant-gray dress . . . Bloom recalls that among her former admirers was the tenor Bartell d'Arcy, who has already figured in "The Dead" in *Dubliners*—a "conceited fellow with his waxedup moustache," who used to take Molly home after practice.

Bartell d'Arcy is probably the only lover Molly has had as a married woman before the arrival of Blazes Boylan, although it's likely that d'Arcy never properly consummated the sexual act with her. In her final monologue, Molly remembers that he kissed her on the choir steps.

From organ pipe to choirboy, A chimed in.

Following this come erotic scenes and suppers (Eroticoculinary, A said) on happy nights with Molly, the Cicerone said, which as Bloom passes by 29 Westmoreland Street, outside Harrison's restaurant, are interrupted by a chance meeting with Mrs. Breen, maiden name Josie Powell, with whom Bloom might have had a relationship if he had not been engaged to Molly. Now weighed down with children, she tells him their mutual friend Mrs. Purefoy ("Beaufoy," thanks to a mistake and masterstroke of Bloom's) has been in the Holles Street maternity hospital for three days, in labor.

Mrs. Breen is married to a poor lunatic (his name, Dennis Breen, is in the 1904 Thom directory) who is obsessed by an anonymous message sent that morning with the cryptic inscription *U.P.*

(which we will try to decipher later on). While she and Bloom are talking, another eccentric, whose name is as long as his bony figure—Cashel Boyle O'Connor Fitzmaurice Tisdall Farrell (a real-life lunatic known in Dublin by the nickname "Endymion")— walks by outside the lampposts carrying "a folded dustcoat, a stick and an umbrella," staring absentmindedly through his monocle as he goes.

While Bloom is talking to Mrs. Breen, he is enveloped in the vapors from the nearby restaurant (a young urchin is breathing them in through the grating), and he realizes he is hungry too.

Bloom's visions turn into provisions, A said.

Yes, B agreed. For example, he notices that Mrs. Breen has three old grapes on her hat, that there are cake crumbs on the gusset of her dress, and a "daub of sugary flour stuck to her cheek" . . . Then he thinks of Mrs. Breen's husband's "oyster eyes" staring at the anonymous message.

And he thinks of the methodical, measured mastication of Mrs. Purefoy's Methodist husband, C said.

The whole chapter is a tragicomedy about food. "Eat or be eaten. Kill! Kill!" Bloom meditates. Everybody here eats and is eaten. A tramp chews his scarred knuckles in the doorway of the Long John, while in another pub, Byrne's, a flea is busy devouring Nosey Flynn, who in turn swallows his own snot. Bloom establishes a list of the strangest things people have been known to eat: Who was it who ate his own dandruff? he wonders. And from there he leaps straight to the Caspian Sea and to caviar . . .

Not to mention the oysters in the Red Bank, B said, which cause him a stab of jealousy when he remembers their aphrodisiacal qualities, although he immediately realizes that Blazes Boylan could not be eating them because there is no *R* in the month.

It's remarkable, remarked Professor Jones, how much seafood and fish are mentioned in this chapter: oysters, lobster, sardines, herring, mackerel, octopus, sturgeon, lemon sole . . .

More than in Homer's sea, A said. From dab to worse.

Raw oysters, like clots of phlegm, said Professor Jones, should get a special mention.

Just so long as you don't get soulful about the sole . . . A said.

I would even wager, Professor Jones insisted, that the word *fish* appears more often in the "Laestrygonians" than *meat*.

It's a tie, B said, consulting the screen:

FISH (6)—MEAT (6)

C said:

The entire chapter is stuffed with the names of foods, with culinary references and food-related metaphors.

Even in people's names, as in the mention of Pepper's ghost, said Professor Jones, or places such as Vinegar Hill.

In this chapter, Joyce's art is like King Midas's in reverse: everything he touches turns to food, A said.

Everything is or could be food, C said. Voracity is the key to this chapter.

Voracity is veracity, A said.

The Cicerone went on:

As he walks past the *Irish Times* a little further on, at 31 Westmoreland Street, Bloom thinks of his secret letter-writer, Martha Clifford, and of another girl who answered his advertisement—her name was Lizzie Twigg—who said that her literary efforts had won the approval of the symbolist poet A.E. (George William Russell, 1867–1935). To Bloom, this disqualified her as being too literary, imagining her as he did with disheveled hair "drinking sloppy tea with a book of poetry."

And just look how Bloom, after visiting several tearooms, sees none other than A.E. himself, talking (of a "twoheaded octopus") to a woman with loose stockings who could well be Lizzie Twigg.

What was the twoheaded octopus? B asked.

Perhaps a symbolist image we cannot make head nor tail of, A ventured.

A.E. tells Lizzie Twigg that one of the two heads spoke with a Scottish accent, Professor Jones said, and in Gaelic *Twig* means "I understand."

Me no understand, B said, frowning. *Twig*?

Yes, *Twig*. One can also *twig*—that is, "understand"—in English (Joyce uses the word in this chapter), and it also refers to the magic or divining wand, Professor Jones explained, glancing across at the Cicerone.

Who, raising his own baton, said no more than that Lizzie Twig was a real flesh-and-blood Dublin poet, a friend of A.E's, and that Bloom contrasts the figures of these two ethereal vegetarian aesthetes (he thinks they have just come out of a vegetarian restaurant) with those of the policemen "sweating Irish stew into their shirts."

Bloom comes to a halt on the corner of Grafton and Nassau Streets. He gazes into the window of Yeats & Son at a pair of field glasses, and wonders about the meaning of the word *parallax*.

Astronomy bursts in on gastronomy, A said.

Bloom is trying to understand the word *parallax*, C said, just as Molly got herself mixed up with the word *metempsychosis*. Both words crop up and trip them up throughout *Ulysses*.

As well as being a leitmotiv in *Ulysses*, Professor Jones said, the word *parallax* defines Joyce's relativism here as concerns the narrative play of his characters' points of view. In astronomy, *parallax* refers to the differences between the apparent and actual positions of a star according to the different points of view from which it is observed.

Bloom is still mooning about, the Cicerone said. He remembers that it was full moon exactly a fortnight before (on May 29, to be exact), and as he, Molly, and Boylan strolled along, the other two touched arms and fingers as they hummed a tune together . . . That's enough, Bloom tells himself, I must try to stop torturing myself. What's done is done, what will be will be. He accepts the fatality and futility of everything, and yet when he passes by the shop windows of Brown and Thomas in Grafton Street, the cascades of ribbons and silks ("A tilted urn poured from its mouth a flood of bloodhued poplin"), stockings and petticoats, drag him back to Molly.

Molly's warm sensuality fries his brains, said A. His appetites get mixed up.

We are going to pause for a minute here too, the Cicerone said, in order to recall a memorable passage that explains Joyce's way of working, and why he was such a musician of language.

Anglo-sax solo . . . said A.

One day in 1918 in Zurich, when Joyce was working on "Laestrygonians," the Cicerone went on, he bumped into his friend, the painter Frank Budgen, on the street. He told him that after a hard day's work he had only written two sentences. He explained that it was not a question of finding the right words, as Flaubert insisted, because he already had them, but of knowing where to put them.

The exact rhythm, B said, and read:

"Perfume of embraces all him assailed. With hungered flesh obscurely, he mutely craved to adore."

"Must eat," says Bloom, and when he reaches Duke Street he decides to go into the Burton restaurant, the Cicerone said, but the smell and sight of the swarm of greedy men eating like animals (the description is worthy of Swift) leads him to leave at once.

Before he does, though, he acts out a scene worthy of Charlie Chaplin, B said. It reveals his delicacy, because in order not to show his disgust, he pretends to be hesitating. He raises two fingers to his lips, and says the person he is looking for is not there.

So instead he goes into Davy Byrne's "moral pub," situated almost opposite at 21 Duke Street. He eats a gorgonzola cheese sandwich with a glass of burgundy. The odd thing is, said the Cicerone, that what used to be the dreadful Burton restaurant became the benign Bailey's restaurant, and it was there that the front door to 7 Eccles Street was on display for many years.

Nosey Flynn, an acquaintance Bloom meets up with in Byrne's, arouses his fears again when he asks after Molly and mentions her manager Boylan. The glass of good wine also stirs up the fire inside him, so that after a few sips and bites of gorgonzola cheese, Bloom's spirits rise. When he sees two flies buzzing, stuck on the windowpane, he starts to remember making love to Molly on a sunlit afternoon hidden beneath ferns on Howth Hill, with Dublin Bay spread out below them. It is one of the central scenes in *Ulysses,* and tells how when he kissed her, she passed a chewed piece of seedcake into his mouth—a moment of intimate communion.

Cupkisscake, A said.

The curves of the wooden bar lead Bloom to think of the curves of naked goddesses in Greek mythology, feeding on nectar, and these thoughts take him on a detour to look at their statues in the National Museum next to the library. Bloom wonders if these sculpted marble women have holes in their behinds, and he decides to go and take a look for himself.

The goddesses represent the ideal world, Professor Jones said. The counterpoint to the dirty reality of existence, the vicious circle that goes from mouth to excrement to earth, then back to food and to the mouth again.

The cycle is interrupted by death, A said. More food for the worms . . .

In what Bloom calls "the very worst hour of the day," C reminded us, he says to himself, "Feel as if I had been eaten and spewed."

That's a feeling that is going to become real when Bloom leaves the pub, A said, and sees a terrier throwing up and then eagerly eating its own sick.

The sight of some lavatory bowls in another shop window brings the chapter's wandering to a close, C said. From mouth to ass.

And Bloom pulls the chain of associations, said A. To dine, don . . .

Yes, and Bloom starts humming and musing once more, C said. This time it's the Commander's aria from *Don Giovanni*.

The dead man coming to supper, exclaimed A. The last one.

Don Giovanni, a cenar teco
M'invitasti.

The Cicerone added that the figure of Don Juan Boylan makes another blazing appearance in daylight (straw hat, tan shoes, trousers turned up in the latest fashion) in Kildare Street, as Bloom is on his way to the library. ("It is. It is," he says, his heart in his mouth.) Bloom decides to avoid him by taking refuge in the museum with his goddesses:

"Safe!"

Passageways

I

A scarlet letter on each white top hat: HELYS.

The sandwich men will not let us forget it is lunchtime, said the Cicerone. Let's look at Y, because he is going to be delayed a little while he takes a hunk of bread out of his foreboard and greedily swallows it as he walks on.

II

In his mind's eye, Bloom sees Molly laughing at the wind, the Cicerone said. He remembers how a gust in Harcourt Road *Brrfoo!* lifted her skirt and boa and almost smothered old Professor Goodwin.

The man who was her accompanist at the time, C said.

But Bloom almost immediately recalls another leg, A said. This time it is a leg of lamb that Molly and he cooked that night of airy arias, when they got home from the concert.

"Winds that Blow from the South" was the title of the song Bartell d'Arcy gave Molly, B said.

III

"Poor Mrs Purefoy!" Bloom sympathizes, thinking of her methodical marital Methodist partner. "Method in his madness," Bloom-Polonius tells himself. "Saffron bun and milk and soda lunch in the educational dairy." (One of the stores selling natural and dietary products run by the Educational Dairy Produce Stores Ltd., the Cicerone explained, where non-alcoholic drinks were also served.) And he imagines the maniacal Purefoy, with his "muttonchop whiskers," "eating with a stopwatch, thirtytwo chews to the minute." His minute menu.

IV

The Laestrygonians in the Burton. When Bloom enters, the stench of men and stale fermented food almost takes his breath away.

"Hungry man is an angry man." The Cicerone pointed his wand at the swarm of swilling humans, those sitting on high stools by the bar, some wearing hats, those sitting at tables "wolfing gobfuls of sloppy food," chucking the food down and choking, the tooth-less man spitting out "halfmasticated gristle," an old man picking his teeth, another greedy customer cramming a knifeful of cab-bage down his throat, one here mopping up his stew gravy with bits of bread, while another one with a dribbled bib takes in more and more, talking to himself with his mouth stuffed full.

V

"Kosher. No meat and milk together." In Byrne's "moral pub," Bloom remembers one of the dietary rules of Judaism, although he himself is not a practicing Jew, said the Cicerone, reminding us once again of the pig's kidneys Bloom had for breakfast.

VI

Bloom's romantic memories last no longer than the coupling of two flies, the Cicerone concluded, pointing to the windowpane with his wand. (Perhaps due to an "insectuous" association, as Mr. Earwicker would say, Professor Jones pointed out.) The climax, when Molly gave herself to him for the first time among the ferns and rhododendrons of Howth, is something she also relives at the end of her monologue. The warmth of the sun on Bloom's palate.

And the taste of Molly on his tongue, A sang softly.

Let's listen to Bloom savoring their communicating kisses, B said:

"Ravished over her I lay, full lips full open, kissed her mouth. Yum. Softly she gave me in my mouth the seedcake warm and chewed."

VII

In Dawson Street around two o'clock, almost at the end of this part of his journey, Bloom helps a blind boy cross Molesworth Street. As Bloom sees everything in this chapter through the filter of food, he notices the stains on the blind boy's coat. He concludes that the boy must slobber his food, and thinks that everything must taste different to him. But let's not lose sight of the blind boy's cane, said the Cicerone, striking the ground with his stick. Its staccato tapping in different Dublin streets will mark the different hours of the novel.

9. SCYLLA AND CHARYBDIS

The comedy of a critical comedy in two acts and an intermission that takes place at two in the afternoon in the office of the director of the Irish National Library in Kildare Street. Taking part in order of appearance are Thomas William Lyster (1855–1922), the library director; Stephen Dedalus; John Eglinton, nom de plume of the librarian William Kirkpatrick Magee (1868–1961); the poet A.E. (George Russell), already glimpsed in the previous chapter; the librarian Richard Irvine Best (1872–1959); and Malachi "Buck" Mulligan.

C (*counting by tapping his pipe on his fingers*): That makes six. I'm afraid there's one missing for a dress rehearsal of *Hamlet*.

PROFESSOR JONES (*eyes rolled up*): The number seven, beloved of the mystical mind and Pythagoreans. The number of creation, of the planets and alchemists . . .

C: "The shining seven," according to a verse by Yeats quoted at the start of this chapter.

B: Yes, it's Bloom who is missing. He appears almost on tiptoe in the middle of this literary piece, then appears and disappears rapidly at the end of the chapter.

A: I would say that Hamlet-Stephen's real ghostly father is Bloom; he is such a ghostly presence we hardly even notice him.

C: Stephen does not yet recognize him as a paternal image.

A: "A father is a necessary evil," Stephen dixit. In fact, relations between father and son are often a comedy of errors, caused above all by mutual ignorance.

C: Stephen recalls his father Simon Dedalus waiting for him on the dock when he came rushing back from Paris and saw that his father was looking kindly on him: "The eyes that wish me well. But do not know me," he adds.

A: But the other phantom member of the family is important too: the mother.

B: The phantom of the mother appears again in this chapter. Stephen remembers telegraphically: "Mother's deathbed. Candle. The sheeted mirror."

C: Stephen is finally going to tell the "ghoststory" his pupils were asking him for that morning.

A: *Hamlet*, a ghost story, as interpreted by Stephen's ghostly theories.

C: "What is a ghost?" Stephen asks, and then gives one of his incisive definitions.

B (*reading*): "One who has faded into impalpability through death, through absence, through change of manners."

C: And he goes on to allude to Shakespeare's absence from his home; he points out that London is as far from Stratford "as corrupt Paris lies from virgin Dublin."

A: Let's not forget that Stephen bought his Hamlet hat in the Latin Quarter . . .

B: Before we talk about ghosts, I would like to focus on a few real details: Stephen's companions treat him with a certain condescension—he is not invited with the rest of them to the meeting the dramatist George Moore is organizing that afternoon, and A.E. has not included Stephen in the anthology of Irish poets he is preparing.

C: That happened to Joyce himself. And we should add that John Eglinton refused to publish *Portrait* in *Dana*, a review he directed.

PROFESSOR JONES: *Stefanos*, king without a crown. When he looks down at his second-feet boots that Mulligan has lent him, he thinks of the cast-off coat of mail that the ghost in *Hamlet* wears.

A: Several ghosts haunt this *mise en abîme* or *mise en scène* of a *Hamlet* of *Hamlet*. Stephen is between the hard place of his own arguments (Kinch-Ockham's double-edged razor . . .) and the rock of reality, between the windmills of the Platonic ideas and ethereal mystic-theosophical theories his aesthete friends tilt at, and the rock of the Aristotelian principles of reality.

C: Stephen listens critically to his companions, and clings on like a red-hot poker to anything he can grasp like a red-hot poker, whatever is nearest to hand, his "casque" and his "sword," which in fact are, and immediately become, his hat and cane.

B: "One hat is one hat," Stephen de La Palice tautologically concludes.

PROFESSOR JONES: One hat is more than one hat. A hat is a female sexual symbol and a cane is a phallic symbol. These are also Stephen's "Scylla and Charybdis." The sexual allusions become more evident when Mulligan appears halfway through the discussion. He is bearing a telegram, and introduces the real intermission in the play.

C: In other words, a play within a play, as in *Hamlet*.

A (*glancing at the screen*): Let's pause here for a commercial break.

```
●○○                    ULYSSES II.9.doc

TITLE: Scylla and Charybdis          ORGAN: Brain

TIME: 2:00–3:00 P.M.                 TECHNIQUE: Dialectic

SCIENCE, ART: Literature             MEANING: Horns of a dilemma

SYMBOL: Stratford, London            CORRESPONDENCES:
                                     Scylla: Aristotle
COLOR: "Local." Every shade, like the enigmatic Mr. W.H.    Charybdis: Plato
The colors of the previous chapters also reappear.
```

CICERONE: In the first chapter, when the Englishman Haines showed an interest in Stephen's theories about *Hamlet*, Mulligan tells him to wait until Kinch has at least three pints of beer inside him. Stephen misses his appointment with Mulligan and Haines at the Ship, and instead of pints of beer he has three whiskies with his journalist friends in two pubs before he turns up at the National Library on an empty stomach to offer his theories on *Hamlet* to a chosen group of aesthetes and librarians. He manages to give A.E. the letter from Mr. Deasy for him to publish in the *Irish Homestead*. Haines has also visited the National Library before Stephen arrived, where he spoke to the librarian Best before going off to buy a book of Celtic folklore.

C: Which means Haines again misses hearing the theory he's so interested in. After much dialectical jousting, as Mulligan had announced while he was shaving, Stephen "proves by algebra that Hamlet's grandson is Shakespeare's grandfather and that he himself is the ghost of his own father."

A: In fact what he proves is that Shakespeare is the son of his work, and the father of all his ancestors . . .

B (*striking herself on the conch-shaped image on her T-shirt*): Ouf! A real family argument . . .

PROFESSOR JONES: Stephen's strange theories about Hamlet were ones that Joyce himself began to evolve in June 1904. It even appears that he first elaborated them on the 16th, and told them to the same librarians and poets assembled in this chapter.

A: Some of them, such as Richard Best, did not in the least like being novel fodder. "I am a living being, not a character in a novel!" was his almost Unamunian or "nivolesque" protest when the BBC wanted to interview him about Joyce's *Ulysses*.

C: Joyce also used the thirteen lectures he gave on *Hamlet* in Trieste in 1912 and 1913 as the basis for this chapter.

PROFESSOR JONES: Contrary to the generally accepted view at that time, Stephen did not think Prince Hamlet was a persona, or mask, of Shakespeare. He thought the playwright was reflected much more in Hamlet's father, as is demonstrated by the fact that he used to play the role of the ghostly father in his own theater. Hamlet is Shakespeare's son Hamnet, who died in early childhood.

B: At the age Rudy would have been in 1904 . . .

PROFESSOR JONES: And the adulterous queen, Hamlet's mother, is in fact Anne Hathaway, Shakespeare's wife, who was eight years older than him, and seduced the young William at the age of eighteen and . . .

A: And gave him a good tumble in the cornfield . . . or rather, as Best says: in a *ryefield*.

PROFESSOR JONES: During Shakespeare's prolonged absence in London, Anne had incestuous relations with two of the playwright's brothers, Edmund and Richard, who are also portrayed and vilified in his works.

C: This question of Anne Hathaway's adultery (Yes, she knew how to seduce: she "hath a way," as Stephen says), interests me more in relation to the theme of adultery in *Ulysses*, because of the parallel with Molly Bloom.

A: Stephen even imagines Anne Hathaway at night making oneiric waters in her chamber pot, just as Molly does or pees.

C: He portrays Anne Hathaway reading cheap literature as Molly does too, rather than *The Merry Wives* . . .

A: Perhaps here Joyce was reproaching someone who did not read his work . . . don't you think . . . ?

B: That's enough. George Russell quite rightly tells Stephen that there's no point prying into the lives of great authors. It's better to scrutinize their works.

PROFESSOR JONES: What is most important in this chapter is that Joyce again puts his finger on the personal wound of infidelity, an autobiographical theme and obsession he had already attempted to explore in another play, *Exiles*.

A: I don't know if he put his digit or his doubt on the wound, but Stephen reaches such absurd conclusions, not even he himself believes them. It is all dialectical dueling by a joker.

C: The most interesting thing about the digressions on "William Shakespeare and company, limited" (*Ulysses* creates its first publisher *avant la lettre*) is what they reveal about *Ulysses*. This chapter is a gloss on *Ulysses* itself.

PROFESSOR JONES: What is especially important is the androgynous conception of intellectual creation.

A: Which Mulligan interrupts with his thrusts, pressing his belly-brow with the hand that is the protagonist of his master-baking comedy.

B: *Love* is the key word in this chapter. And the question is again asked: What is the word known to all men?

C: And when he refers to Shakespeare's seduction by Anne Hathaway, Stephen wonders when it will happen to him, and with whom.

A: As Stephen leaves the library with Mulligan, Bloom passes between them. "The wandering jew," as Mulligan calls him. And in the portico Stephen relives his premonitory dream of an Oriental offering him a cream-fruit melon.

PROFESSOR JONES: Stephen is Scylla, the monster on his Aristotelian rock. Mulligan is Charybdis, the whirlpool. Bloom succeeds in passing between the two of them.

C: Yet there is more than one "Scylla and Charybdis" in the chapter. For example, Stephen has to find the middle way between the bodiless soul of the theosophists and aesthetes like A.E., and the soulless body of the materialist Mulligan.

PROFESSOR JONES: One last personal interpretation: as we know, Bloom is Ulysses, and the six men who vie with each other dialectically in the library are Ulysses' six companions—I won't mention their names here—whom Scylla devoured with its six mouths.

A: (*moving his head to right and left*): *Se non è vero* . . .

B: We should concentrate more on the "dark back" that walks in front of Stephen and Mulligan: the step of a Leo-pard.

Passageways

I

C: The librarian Best refers to a prose poem by Mallarmé about *Hamlet*. He quotes in French: "*il se promène . . .* don't you know, *reading the book of himself.*" He could equally well have recalled that Mallarmé calls Hamlet: "This walker in a labyrinth of agitation and grievance . . ."

B: And Best writes in the air the poster for the performance of *Hamlet* in a provincial town that Mallarmé refers to:

HAMLET

ou

LE DISTRAIT

Pièce de Shakespeare

A: A play by Shakespeare and about Shakespeare . . .

C: Stephen says later on that "We walk through ourselves," and when it comes down to it, every journey is an appointment with oneself.

II

C: Stephen imagines the scene with the ghost. He describes the actor advancing in shadow.

A: A tall man with a bass voice.

B: It's the ghost of Hamlet's father as represented by Shakespeare: *Hamlet, I am thy father's spirit.*

A: But in fact he is not speaking to the son of his spirit, Prince Hamlet, but to the son of his body, Hamnet, who died in childhood.

PROFESSOR JONES: Hamnet Shakespeare (1585–1596).

A: One ghost talking to another.

PROFESSOR JONES: All that is well and good. But Stephen's quotation from *Hamlet* is incorrect. That "Hamlet" is not in the original. The ghost simply says: *I am thy father's spirit.*

C: In fact, Bloom had already made the same mistake back in the "Laestrygonians."

III

C: The library as cemetery . . .

A: Stephen thinks of the mummies of knowledge, in the knowledge buried in books that was once enclosed in living brains.

B (*reads*): "Coffined thoughts around me, in mummycases,

embalmed in spice of words. Thoth, god of libraries, a birdgod, moonycrowned."

IV

CICERONE: The telegram that Stephen, or rather as he signed it, *Dedalus*, sent from the College Green post office to Malachi Mulligan.

C: He addressed it to the Ship Inn in Lower Abbey Street, where they were supposed to meet.

B: Smiling, Mulligan reads it out loud: "The sentimentalist is he who would enjoy without incurring the immense debtorship for a thing done."

C: A quotation from the novel, *The Ordeal of Richard Feverel* (1859), by George Meredith.

PROFESSOR JONES: The quotation in the telegram is from the revised 1875 edition.

B: This telegram leads us back to Paris and another one which led Stephen to return to Dublin.

A: A telegram with an erratum: *Nother*. Bringing the ghost back from the other world, the *nether world*, or rather *nother world* . . .

V

B (*reads*): "A patient silhouette waited, listening."

CICERONE: Bloom comes to the library to consult back issues of the *Kilkenny People* newspaper for 1903, where he is hoping to find the image for the Keyes ad.

A: While the others speechify about Shakespeare, he is waiting for the library director's permission, and listens intently.

C: He has already satisfied his visual curiosity by going to take a look at the Venus in the museum. Mulligan says he saw him there. Now Bloom listens in the library.

A: The Hebrew faced with highbrows . . .

VI

CICERONE: Mulligan's empty hand.

A: Another mount of Venus . . .

PROFESSOR JONES: Incapable of true intellectual creation, Mulligan makes up an obscene parody. After all the intellectual onanism of the empty discussions that represent the sterility of Dublin cultural life, Mulligan offers his obscene proposal.

C: "In sweetly varying voices Buck Mulligan read his tablet:

Everyman His own Wife
or
A Honeymoon in the Hand
(a national immorality in three orgasms)
by
Ballocky Mulligan

10. THE WANDERING ROCKS

The leaflet that Bloom threw to the seagulls from O'Connell Bridge two chapters earlier and is now floating down the Liffey, Professor Jones said, is both a wandering rock and the ship of the Argonauts.

And the river is a labyrinth, C said. It runs through another labyrinth: Dublin.

Everything in this chapter is a labyrinth, C said, and appropriately, the technique is labyrinthine.

A labyrinth inside a labyrinth, A insisted. Because in a labyrinthine way, the chapter is at the center of another labyrinth or "liberinth": *Ulysses*.

Dedalus of Dedaluses . . . B said.

Yes, the whole Dedalus family makes its appearance through this chapter, A said. Stephen, his mother, his sisters.

This chapter is a model in the form of a jigsaw puzzle for *Ulysses* as a whole, C said.

It consists of nineteen sections, Professor Jones said. Although some commentators say it has eighteen sections and a coda. It seems to me that "Wandering Rocks" is made up of seventeen mini-episodes, equal to the number of episodes in *Ulysses*, not counting this one, and framed by Father Conmee's journey at the beginning and that of the Viceroy at the end. So the spiritual power—the Church—and the temporal power—the British government—provide the framework for the chapter, for Dublin and Ireland in general.

What we do know, said C, is that Joyce carefully traced the itineraries of Father Conmee and the Viceroy on a map of Dublin.

He also carefully traced, with compass, ruler, and watch in hand, B said, the paths of the fifty characters who appear and disappear on the streets of Dublin.

As they crisscross the city, these characters, who make up almost the entire cast of the novel, create an intricate labyrinth on top of the labyrinth of streets, A said.

It is almost like a board game, C said. A game of chess where the pieces are the people on the checkerboard of the city.

While a mysterious Master moves the pieces . . . A said.

Like the one who appears in Section 8. B opened his copy: "From a long face a beard and gaze hung on a chessboard."

That is Parnell's brother, C said. Mulligan points him out to Haines in the D.B.C. (Dublin Bakery Company or *damn bad cakes*) tearoom of Section 16, situated at 33 Dame Street.

The revelations and knowledge emerge gradually, said A, as so often is the case in cities.

For example, B said, the anonymous constable who salutes Father Conmee in the first section is 57C in the second section, isn't he?

It's quite likely, A said. Sometimes if we miss a fact or detail we can get lost in the city.

Joyce's labyrinth is also one of ambiguity, of ambiguous identities, said C. For example, Bloom the dentist has nothing to do with Leopold Bloom. Nor should we confuse Ben Dollard with Dollard the printer, nor Father Cowley with Alderman Cowley . . .

And as also happens in a city, our first impressions can sometimes be completely wrong. For example, when M'Coy and Lenehan see Bloom, in Section 9, in front of a bookseller's stall, they think he is looking for an astronomy textbook, because that is one of his passions. But in fact he is after erotic novels for Molly.

And we get more erotic literature soon afterwards from Lenehan the sports reporter, B said. When he describes a trip with Molly in a swaying cab.

Really graphic pornography if you think of the gestures he makes to describe how big her breasts were, A said. He becomes really excited: "His hands moulded ample curves of air."

All the while Bloom is running his fingers over printed words, the opulence of paper, B said.

The pleasures of reading, A said. The sweetness of the solitary sin of reading . . .

And while in the background, under Merchant's Arch, we see the dark back of Bloom bending over erotic books, B said, in the foreground we see Boylan "reading" the carnal lines of the girl in Thornton's fruit and flower shop at 63 Grafton Street, and touching the ripe pears.

In that fifth section, A said, Boylan's eyes—and those of the curious reader—peer down the front of the blond fruit shop assistant's dress. A foretaste of Molly's succulent, forbidden fruits . . .

Stephen also reads, in Section 13, a book of magic formulas (for example, "How to win a woman's love") in a book he buys in Clohissey's bookshop at 10–11 Bedford Row, said B.

A trait that Stephen and Bloom share is that they prefer books to the works themselves, said A.

In Section 7 there is another reader who likes to daydream, B said. That's Miss Dunne, Boylan's secretary, who has just hidden a copy of *The Woman in White* in her desk drawer.

And then she types . . . tip . . . tap . . . the date of *Ulysses*, A said.

"16 June 1904," said B. I suspect that Miss Dunne is "Martha Clifford."

She could be, C said. She also commits a really significant mistake or *lapsus*. After she puts the Wilkie Collins novel away, she wonders: "Is he in love with that one, Marion?" But there is no Marion in *The Woman in White*. Instead there is a Marian, with an *A*, Marian Halcombe.

Does Martha Clifford know who Henry Flower really is? B asked.

It could be part of the game of mirrors that Joyce likes to play, said A. Without knowing it, Boylan and Bloom in some way share another woman.

The secretary and the secret correspondent, C said.

At the end of this section, B said, Boylan calls his secretary from the fruit shop, and she gives him the message that Lenehan will be waiting for him at four in the Ormond Hotel.

We'll be there, A said. Although I think Boylan has a more important appointment at that time.

And at the Ormond we'll also meet the blind piano tuner Bloom helped across the road at the end of the "Laestrygonians." He's here again in Sections 17 and 19, B said.

All the different activities in the nineteen sections sometimes occur at the same time in different parts of the city, said C.

But time and space are interpolated, Professor Jones said. So are the different activities.

They crisscross and are juxtaposed, A pointed out. This can lead to ironic and comic effects, or give rise to ambiguities. Ambiguity through contiguity . . .

Sometimes it's hard to establish the chronological order of the episodes, Professor Jones said. But we can follow their spatial disposition on a map of Dublin. If we take their proximity into account, we can establish the following sequence: 1, 2, 3, 4, 5, 12, 17, 6, 7, 8, 9, 10, 11, 13, 14, 15, 16, 18, and 19.

A model kit, A said. Or it might be easier to think of counterpoint technique.

What is striking is the game of synchronization and desynchronization, said C. For example, in the second section we see a "generous white arm" (Molly Bloom's arm, as we later discover) throwing a coin to a one-legged sailor from a house window (at 7 Eccles Street); yet in Section 3, the sailor is just starting to go down Eccles Street, and it is only at the end of that section that the woman's hand throws him a coin.

In Section 3, we see the card advertising *Unfurnished Apartments* fall from a window in Molly's house, A said. It reappears at the same sash window in Section 9.

Molly is the one who props it back up, said B. At about a quarter past three, more or less when Bloom acquires *The Sweets of Sin* in Section 10.

Another curious thing, worthy of a person of multiple curiosities, A said, is the multiple points of view, the combination of close-ups and bird's eye or Icarus's eye views, using a truly cinematographic technique, or those of the lame devil Asmodeus lifting up house-roofs.

The boot that steps on the phlegm in Section 10, said A, or in a flashback, a hand nailed to the table by a dagger.

Or the fists of the two boxers that the young Dignam boy and his identical reflection the young Dignam boy stare at from the two side windows of the shop front.

Let's look at some of those images, a sort of trailer for the chapter, the Cicerone announced, entering the iridescent room without glancing at the diagram that flashed on the screen.

ULYSSES II.10.doc

TITLE: The Wandering Rocks	ORGAN: Blood
SETTING: Streets of Dublin	TECHNIQUE: Labyrinth
TIME: 2:55–3:40 P.M.	MEANING: Hostile environment
SCIENCE, ART: Mechanics	CORRESPONDENCES:
	Bosphorus: River Liffey
SYMBOL: Citizens	European Shore: The Viceroy
	Asian Shore: Father Conmee
COLOR: Colors of the rainbow	Symplegades (Wandering Rocks): Groups of Dubliners

Joyce was wrong, or was trying to wrongfoot us when he said that the wandering rocks are the inhabitants of Dublin, Professor Jones insisted. On the contrary, the inhabitants are victims caught between two powerful rocks: the Catholic Church, founded as we know on a rock, and the equally rocklike and petrified British Empire.

"O, rocks!" said B, imitating Molly.

What symplegades! A said.

The two masters Stephen referred to at the start of *Ulysses*, Professor Jones said.

The Jesuit Father John Conmee (1847–1910), the Cicerone explained, headmaster of Clongowes Wood College (1885–1891) during the years when Stephen (and Joyce himself) were pupils there, leaves his residence at the priest's house in Upper Gardiner Street in the northern part of central Dublin, and travels some two and a half miles on foot and by tram, until he reaches the O'Brien Institute orphanage in Artane, in the northeast of the city. He is carrying a letter of recommendation from Martin Cunningham for Patrick Dignam to be received into that institution. The Viceroy leaves his official residence in Phoenix Park, on the western outskirts of the city, to inaugurate a charity tombola at the Mirus Bazaar.

In real life, the inauguration of the Mirus Bazaar took place a few days earlier, on May 31.

The two itineraries, and those of the people they meet on the way, are full of ironic and satirical touches, C said.

The irony surfaces above all in Father Conmee's journey, A said. It could be said that the Viceroy's cavalcade is seen through the "savage lens"—both comic and distorting—of Cashel Boyle O'Connor Fitzmaurice Tisdall, who at the end of the journey passes in front of Finn's Hotel, from where perhaps he was spotted by a young chambermaid called Nora . . .

On the corner of Haddington Road, B said, we see the two astonished ladies with their umbrella and bag of cockles (precisely eleven) whom Stephen had seen in "Proteus."

Joyce tells us that the meaning of this chapter is the "hostile environment," Professor Jones said. The lack of charity, of love for one's neighbor, or for justice is made obvious throughout the chapter. Father Conmee is concerned with an orphan, perhaps because recommended by the "useful" and attentive lawyer Cunningham, someone who might be able to offer him or the Society further help, and yet he is incapable of giving the one-legged sailor any change from his own pocket. Stephen is touched by the desperate straits Dilly and his other sisters are in, but he does not give them a penny of the money he is going to spend so carelessly in a few hours' time. The sense of fraternity, not merely the Christian one, has been lost *tout court*. So the path taken by the Church (represented by the Jesuit John Conmee's journey) shows the degradation of the Christian virtue of charity. Father Conmee is unable not only to share his cape or mantle with a poor man, but he cannot share his crown either.

What a lack of compassion, said A.

But it is not really his money, C objected. It belongs to the Society. And besides, since he only has one silver crown and has to take the tram to reach the orphanage, any generous gesture would have been of little practical use.

That's a typically "Jesuitical" argument, Professor Jones protested. Joyce portrays his former teacher and protector in a very sympathetic way, but in the end the image we have of him is of a Jesuit who is a diplomat, a snob, something of a dreamer, good on the surface but basically ineffectual.

I'm more interested in the suggestive scene at the end of the first section, said A. The one where Father Conmee is busy reading his breviary by Clongowes field and blesses the young man and woman who emerge from a hedge looking embarrassed.

The significant detail, B said: she takes a twig from her skirt . . .

As we learn four chapters later, said C, the young man was Vincent Lynch, a friend of Stephen's.

He is another reader of the sweets of sin, A said. Father Conmee was reading a page in his breviary that started with the Hebrew letter *sin*.

The letter *sin* of a passage from Psalm 119: "Princes also did sit and speak against me: but thy servant did meditate in thy statutes," Professor Jones quoted. But if the mother church has failed, so too will the paternalist government. In the pomp of state, as represented by the Viceroy, there is a blindness and sometimes frivolous view of the needs and misery of Ireland.

The only blindness I see, A said, is that of the young man outside Broadbent's fruiterers at the end of the last section.

Nor does the Viceroy see, also on Lower Mount Street, Professor Jones continued, the man in the macintosh eating dry bread . . . and Joyce misleads us yet again when he has the Viceroy cross the Royal Canal Bridge when in fact it is the bridge over the Grand Canal.

To a viceroy, all bridges are royal, A said.

Ouf! the Cicerone puffed, and moved off quickly, tapping the floor with his stick, raising it as we passed various images.

Passageways

I

A merry heart goes all the way, said the Cicerone ironically, and the one-legged sailor grunts a few notes outside the Sisters of Charity Convent in Upper Gardiner Street. He holds his cap out to Father Conmee as he goes past, but the priest only has a silver crown on him, and so can only give him his blessing.

On the corner of Mountjoy Square, Father Conmee stops three boys from the Belvedere primary school and gets them to post a letter from him to the father provincial, pointing out the mailbox on the corner of Fitzgibbon Street to them.

II

Mr. Denis Maginni, dance teacher, a popular figure in Dublin, dressed in his striking and characteristic outfit of top hat, slate-colored frockcoat, tight-fitting lavender trousers, canary-yellow gloves, and pointed patent boots respectfully made room for Lady Maxwell on the corner of Dignam's Court, close to where the Thom directory tells us she really lived, at 36 Great George's Street North.

III

At Newcomen Bridge over the Royal Canal, Father John Conmee catches a tram toward Dollymount (a town some three and a half miles northeast of Dublin) and sits in a corner seat. The conductor gives him his change: exactly four shillings, a sixpenny piece, and five one penny coins. The gentleman in glasses sitting opposite Father Conmee looks down at the floor after talking to a woman Father Conmee takes to be his wife, and then she opens her mouth and sketches a yawn.

The marvelous sketch is catching, B said, reading: "She raised her small gloved fist, yawned ever so gently, tiptapping her small gloved fist on her opening mouth and smiled tinily, sweetly."

IV

When Joyce was writing the "Wandering Rocks" in Zurich, the Cicerone explained, in the evenings he used to play a board game called *Labyrinth* with his daughter Lucia.

At that time Joyce had a very romantic-looking beard, B said. A beard and an intent gaze hanging over a board . . .

V

At the same time as Corny Kelleher in the doorway of his funeral parlor (the one in charge of Dignam's burial) sends "a silent jet of hayjuice arching from his mouth," Molly's generous white arm sends a coin out of her window to the one-legged sailor.

When it comes down to it, said Professor or Preacher Jones, it is only the "sinning" adulteress Molly and her non-practicing Jewish husband Leopold (who puts five shillings into the collection for Dignam's family) who practice Christian charity.

And Andalusian Molly's lover chews the stem of the red carnation that the blonde in the florist's gave him, the Cicerone continued.

A florist's called Thornton, A said. No carnation without a thorn?

VI

Elijah is coming, intoned the Cicerone, and the wandering leaflet, after coming and going up and down the Liffey with the tide, tiny crumpled boat which in Section 4 passed under the Loopline Bridge, went on past hulls and anchor chains on Sir John Rogerson's Quay heading westward, until at the end of Section 17 it has floated beyond Wapping Street, past Benson's ferry and the three-master *Rosevean* that Stephen had glimpsed from the beach at the end of "Proteus."

Tom Kernan, commercial agent and tea merchant, with proud bearing as befits a retired officer from India, is walking along James Street in an easterly direction and at No. 48 has time to admire himself in the mirror at Peter Kennedy the hairdresser's doorway. A little further on, almost in Thomas Street West, the glint of the sun on a car windshield leads him to doubt the identity of a passerby he knew or did not know (isn't it Ned Lambert's brother?).

The windshield almost shaves off Tom Kernan's grizzled moustache, said A. In 1904, motorcars did not yet have windshields.

I think this is the only motorcar in *Ulysses*, C said.

Was it a deliberate anachronism? B asked.

But the Cicerone was drawn to other images. For example, that of Almidano Artifoni, Stephen's former music teacher, and the poster for the enchanting English singer and comedienne Marie Kendall (1873–1964) superimposed on the old print Stephen sees in the window of Clohissey's bookshop in Bedford Row: two heavyweight boxers lightweight in their clothing, holding up their bare fists.

They were the North American John Heenan and the Englishman Tom Sayers, Professor Jones explained. They fought on April 17, 1860 at Farnborough, England, in a bout that lasted thirty-seven rounds. The fight was—

A counterpoint of images, A interrupted him impatiently, which leads us to the concert or musically disconcerting image of the next chapter.

The fight was a tie, Professor Jones insisted: "heroes' hearts."

VIII

The Cicerone told us:

At the intersection of Dame Street and College Green, the lawyer John Henry Menton (a former admirer of Molly's, who during Dignam's funeral scarcely deigns to look at Bloom) watches the Viceroy and his retinue pass by with his "oyster eyes," holding a fat gold watch in his fat left hand. At 116 Grafton Street, on Ponsonby the bookseller's corner, H and slightly behind him E, L, Y and S stop to admire the prancing horse and carriages. By the provost's wall at Trinity College, Blazes Boylan strides gaily by, "his straw hat at a rakish angle," offering the three ladies in the Viceroy's entourage an insolently admiring gaze and the red carnation between his lips.

11. THE SIRENS

Bar in music and bar in a bar, barked the Cicerone, raising his wand to sharpen our hearing

(We have to listen attentively, B reminded us. With in-tension.)

And hear the drumming of the iron horses' hooves together with Lydia Douce and Mina Kennedy, two pretty barmaids

(Barmaids and mermaids, sea sirens and girls in a pub . . . A went on.)

Whose heads appear together, bronze

(Bronzed or even a little sunburned was the enchanting Miss Douce, enchantress of the unwary, B said, whom she amazed with her mermaid-white skin on the sands at Rostrevor during her recent holidays there)

And gold

(A gold mine, this blond Mina, A said in minor key: *Minor* Kennedy . . .)

Bronze brunette and blond gold at the blind on a window of the bar at the Hotel Ormond, watching the Viceroy and his entourage go by.

Non sequitur . . . Professor Jones said. Occasionally the answers precede the questions during the game of counterpoint in this complex (or did he say convex?) chapter, which Joyce called a *fuga per canonem*, although the rules of music are not always respected or respectable.

The virtuosity of this chapter is also shown by its orchestral composition: it starts with the vibrant sound of the brass section, and fades away with a wind instrument.

It also has an operatic air to it, Professor Jones continued, as well as something of the unfinished symphony. For example, the fifty-seven themes of the chapter's opening are incomprehensible (and during the First World War, Joyce had problems with British military censorship when he sent this chapter from Switzerland to England)—or at least not fully comprehensible until we read it through again. *Da capo.*

Da capolavoro, said A. Music, maestro.

As Bloom so rightly thinks, B reminded us, "Beauty of music you must hear twice."

Back to *Ulysses*! Encore, you listeners, hissed A, glancing at the man with the Macintosh, who seemed to be entirely self-absorbed, listening to his own silence.

We've reached the hour of the ear, said A. Time can also be measured by the metronome.

Tick tock, B tacked on. And by the tapping of the cane belonging to the blind piano tuner who forgot his fork on the piano at the Ormond and returns to fetch it. Tap tap tap.

<table>
<tr><td>TITLE: The Sirens</td><td>ORGAN: Ear</td></tr>
<tr><td>SETTING: Concert Room, bar, and restaurant at the Ormond Hotel</td><td>TECHNIQUE: Fuga per canonem</td></tr>
<tr><td></td><td>MEANING: Sweet deceit</td></tr>
<tr><td>TIME: 3:40–4:30 P.M.</td><td>CORRESPONDENCES:</td></tr>
<tr><td>SCIENCE, ART: Music</td><td>Sirens: Barmaids
Island: Bar</td></tr>
<tr><td>SYMBOL: Barmaids</td><td></td></tr>
<tr><td>COLOR: Coral</td><td></td></tr>
</table>

(ULYSSES II.11.doc)

And by the jingling trot of Boylan's tilbury* too, A said, on its way to Eccles Street to rehearse the next concert at a little after four in Molly's bedroom, and a certain jangling of the brass quoits also puts the bed from Gibraltar to the test, toccata and fugue, while the infelicitous feline Leopold scratches and remembers and scrapes a catgut thong.

While the verbal fugue flows on like an underground brook of Bach and develops its meandering serpentine theme (Miss Douce will wet herself, yes she will, Miss Douce laughs so much), surrounding with its current the two sirens stranded at the Hotel

---

* Perhaps we should explain what this typically Irish tilbury, or "jaunting car," is like, said Professor Jones. It is an open carriage with two wheels where the driver is up front and the passengers sit along the sides, their backs to each other.

Ormond bar, on the north bank of the Liffey, at 8 Upper Ormond Quay, Bloom is on his way to the hotel clutching his copy of *The Sweets of Sin* (for Molly! a North American erotic wet dream); we can see him in the distance, he's the man in black crossing Essex Bridge (better known as Grattan Bridge), said the Cicerone, holding out his wand, that's him, when Simon Dedalus, Stephen's father, enters the all-singing, all-dancing bar with the barmaid sirens, that's him, with his Henry Flower nom de plume, walking to Daly's shop at 1 Ormond Quay Upper to buy two sheets of vellum paper and two envelopes—better safe than sorry—on which to write his love letter to Martha Clifford. As he leaves Daly's, he catches sight of the tilted Panama in the distance on Essex Bridge; that's Boylan, galloping towards the Ormond bar where Lenehan is waiting impatiently for him, the same destination as Bloom, who eats his heart out along with liver and mashed potatoes, an early dinner or a late lunch at four in the afternoon, bread and a glass of cider help the pain go down.

One by one the performers turn up at the bar, with its siren song. They are distributed as follows: in the room known as the Concert Room and in the bar, we find the barmaids Miss Douce, she of the cascading laughter who plays so softly at the polished beerpull, and Miss Kennedy, blond as lager beer, who strokes the gold of her hair and does not see her colleague snap, *Sonnez!* her elastic garter against her thigh, for the intent ears of Boylan, who tosses down his glass of sloe gin in the bar with Lenehan, then rushes excitedly out to catch the jingling tilbury, better late than never, on his way to his appointment at Eccles, *La cloche!* at number 7 Eccles Street.

Not to mention the aforementioned Lenehan, who gulps down his bitter, Boylan's cheap treat, and continues to admire lustfully and jocularly his "Rose of Castile," Miss Douce's robust black satin bust. Also in the bar are a bootblack and a busboy, who serves cups of tea to the two barmaids and drums imperthnthntly on his tray; likewise, the solicitous solicitor Mr. Lidwell* who is unctuously soliciting Miss Douce. Also there are the smooth and stout Tom Kernan, two anonymous beer drinkers, the "barreltoned" Ben Dollard, and the skinny "Father" Bob Cowley (who hung up his habits a long while ago), all of them accompanying Simon Dedalus, with his fine tenor voice (the son's a chip off the old block) on the recently tuned piano.

In the next-door dining room are the deaf waiter Pat, Leopold Bloom, and Richie Goulding, Stephen's maternal uncle. The two men eat, say nothing, and listen. And see. Bloom catches another glimpse of Boylan, who is going to be late for his appointment, to the long-suffering husband's bewilderment; he is suffering and enjoying, or "suffjoying," in a masochistic way, imagining his imminent betrayal. He *nodes* and *disnodes* his cuckold's horns, an elastic band between his fingers as he eats his mashed potatoes and liver and hears Ben Dollard sing, remembering how ridiculous the singer looked in that wretched dress-suit he borrowed from the Blooms for a concert, the trouser legs like legs of ham, and has a happy memory of Molly's thighs as she collapsed with laughter on the bed, legs in the air. She too used to wet herself with laughter. Bloom wanders down memory lane, rolling in the

---

* Another real-life character, Professor Jones said. He was the lawyer who was not of much help to Joyce in his drawn-out legal battles over the publication of *Dubliners* with the Dublin press Maunsel and Co.

rhododendrons at Howth, and while Cowley sings *M'Appari* a boat appears, a sail above the waves . . .

Everything is lost, a sad aria for a fatalistic Bloom, who accepts that what will be, will be; easier to hold back the sea, the husband says to himself, impotently, to plough the sea, he says, martyring himself; but Dedalus's serene song makes him think again of Martha, another siren he runs no risks with, better to write to her from this other Ormond, pretending he is composing a commercial letter. Bloom asks deaf Pat for a pen, ink, a pad, and a blotter. "Remember write Greek ees," he reminds himself. "No, change that ee." Write Hεnry with that artistic Greek *E*. Looking at the address on the blotting pad (didn't he forget one Greek *E*?), he has an idea for a detective story. But time and the jingling tilbury continue to fly, and at 7 Eccles Street the tick tock is about to sound, the penetrating cock cock of Bloom's misfortune, which this time reminds him of Paul de Kock, the writer with the French *poil de coq* for a name, or perhaps just the name of a cock, that tick tock which makes his heart stop. He will soon be old and defeated, he tells himself. As he stands up he thinks, "Soap feeling rather sticky behind"; he leaves his newspaper-baton and perhaps by the door as he goes out sees the burial of the sardine that the widower Dedalus's sad eyes had been contemplating. An emblematic image for the lonely Bloom.

"Under the sandwichbell lay on a bier of bread one last, one lonely, last sardine of summer."

In order to escape from another siren—one he has known in the past—Bloom stops to look in a shopwindow on the corner of Arran Street, then takes advantage of the fact that there is no one around and a tram is going by *kran, kran* to tranquilly get rid of his wind.

Something that was unbearable, C said, for delicate souls like Virginia Woolf. She complained to Lytton Strachey of the vulgarities in *Ulysses*: "First there's a dog that p's—then there's a man that forths . . ."

She didn't care much for the "other world" of Joyce's scatology either, Professor Jones said.

But you have to listen to the end of the fugue, said A, in the key of *fart*. The *do di peto*.

And someone (the Cicerone? The man with the Macintosh?) repeated it *au pet de la lettre*:

Pprrpffrrppffff.

Passageways

I

The musical opening of "The Sirens" might at first sight or hearing seem like an incongruous list, C said. But its motifs or themes become clearer and better defined as we progress through the reading of the episode, and we catch all its sense or "nonsense" if we read it again.

Music to be reread, B reminded us.

Here we have, said the Cicerone, pointing with his wand, the iron hooves of the cavalcade, Bloom's blue flower, blond Mina Kennedy's gold hair which she coils and uncoils, the garter that the snappy but sweet Miss Douce snaps for Boylan, the throbbing rose of Castile at her satin bosom, the Viceroy's cab magnified into a state coach, the hard cash Boylan lays on the bar when the cuckold clock strikes the fateful four in the afternoon, the undulating veil over the waves of a print in front of which Cowley sang, the horn, oh yes the horn, not exactly of plenty ("Got the horn or what?" Lenehan asks when Boylan rushes out of the Ormond to go put horns on Bloom), the thrush that warbles too late in the ballad, the knife Bloom uses to cut his thick slices of liver, the horn-shaped seashell through which we hear the receding waves (there is an abundance of marine images in this episode), Miss Douce's tremulous giggles when Big Ben Dollard sings the patriotic ballad "The Croppy Boy," the rolled-up copy or baton of the *Freeman* of Bloom-Flower who ends up feeling gloomy: "I feel so sad today," in his P.S. to Martha Clifford. Alone. *Più forte*. Pff.

II

Bronze next to Gold, Lydia Douce's head next to Mina Kennedy's, the two barmaids stare out of the Ormond at the Viceroy's cavalcade. Miss Kennedy sees and admires Lady Dudley seated next to His Excellency, but Miss Douce is more interested in the man with the top hat in the second carriage, the aide-de-camp Gerald Ward, and sees or imagines that he turns to look at her, at sweet Miss Douce, who is also the most beautiful, the most seductive of sirens. From her vantage point, sweet Douce also sees Bloom outside Moulang's pipe shop at 31 Wellington Quay, with his *The Sweets of Sin* clutched to his chest.

III

The two sirens about to take their cheerful four o'clock tea, protected behind the bar counter (we never see their mermaids' tails, said the Cicerone), smooth down their black satin blouses. Miss Douce unbuttons hers to show her sunburned neck to Miss Kennedy, then gets up to examine it in the mirror with gilded lettering on it: Cantrell and Cochrane's. This is a British beverage company, the Cicerone explained, then went on to tell us about the laughing sirens' tea as they swallowed their hysterical laughter, laughing at Bloom, and Miss Douce almost chokes on her tea and laughter, imagining herself married to the greasy, unattractive fellow. The pair of them laugh until they're doubled up, until they're exhausted.

And Miss Douce all wet, C recalled.

When I makes tea, I makes water, A mimicked mockingly.

IV

The Cicerone said:

Here comes the suitor with his straw hat tilted at a rakish angle and his tan shoes like a dandy. To Bloom's surprise, his tilbury pulls up outside the Ormond: Bloom knows he has an appointment with Mrs. Marion Bloom at this time. Bloom the cautious black cat slips between the tilbury and the bar window to meet up with Richie Goulding. He goes with him into the hotel restaurant. From there he can watch the bar next door without being seen.

As he enters, Boylan touches his straw hat to Miss Kennedy, who smiles at him. But Miss Douce gives him an even bigger smile, smoothing down her hair, her satin bodice, and her rose, just for him.

V

The Cicerone said:

Through the bar doorway, Bloom sees the pointed horn, what a lovely seashell, that sweet Lydia Douce brought back as a souvenir of her holidays in Rostrevor. Coquettishly she places it against the ear of the solicitor George Lidwell, who is all ears, then she lifts it to her own ear which is also a shell with its mother-of-pearl lobe—her underwater charms. "What are the wild waves saying?" Lidwell asks the sweet Lydia, and, ever the scientist, Bloom has already reflected that it is not the sea they hear, but the flow of blood, our own red sea.

VI

Bloom is about to leave the Ormond when the *barreltone* Dollard, roused by drink, his downfall, starts to sing the emotive patriotic ballad about the boy who is a martyr to the cause of Irish independence. Bloom, who has already been admiring sweet Douce face-to-face in the mirror (and has even asked himself for a moment, poor fool, if she might not be his secret correspondent . . .)

exits accompanied by the tune, past the throbbing rose in the satin bosom, past the caressing hand, past the unstoppered stoppers, past the bottles and glasses, past his final reflection: "I feel so sad today."

VII

On Ormond Quay, Bloom sees the last siren of the chapter coming towards him: "A frowsy whore with black straw sailor hat," a woman who once upon a time he was on the verge of being seduced by, whom he allows to carry on past him while, in the window of Lionel Marks's antique shop, he contemplates a melodeon, which gives Bloom breath enough to break wind as he reads on a print the last words of Robert Emmet (1778–1803), an Irish hero executed following a failed insurrection. Thus it is that rhetoric and pedantic oratory end up as popular music.

Pprrpffrrppffff.

12. THE CYCLOPS

Two eyes see better than one, A added, pushing his steel-rimmed dark glasses onto his nose with his forefinger as he made to enter the green room.

Yes, C said. That is the simple conclusion* of "Cyclops."

In the land of the blind, the one-eyed man is king, said A.

"Cyclops" also tells us that all narrow-minded nationalism is blind, C said.

And stupid, A added. Blinkered jingoism.

Yes, C said, in "Cyclops" Joyce satirized intolerant nationalism, xenophobia, chauvinism, fanaticism, and the intolerance of some Irish radical groups such as the Fenians, caricatured here in the figure of the Citizen.

---

* "Concussion," wrote Professor Jones as a footnote.

Citizen Cain, A suggested. A murderous fellow.

"Citizen Cossack," Professor Jones said, or at least that's what A understood, and then echoed back:

Cossack?

Cusack, said Professor Jones, thumbing his notebook. His model was Michael Cusack (1847–1906), the founder of the Gaelic Athletic Association, dedicated to promoting and re-introducing ancient Irish sports. He was a violent nationalist who called himself "Citizen Cusack."

Joyce knew him personally, A said. And, as one might expect, had little time for him.

As well as fanatical nationalism, in this chapter Joyce satirized the slanders and gossip of a squalid Dublin stubbornly shut in on itself, the prisoner of its own prejudices, said C.

Bad-mouthing, A said, that gets worse with every mouthful . . .

It's fitting that we see poor Denis Breen again in this chapter, said B. He's still walking through Dublin followed by his ever-patient wife, heavy tomes under his arm, ready to take legal action against the anonymous sender of the postcard.

In the "Laestrygonians," Bloom suspected Alf Bergan and Richie Goulding, A said. And in this chapter, in Kiernan's pub, it is precisely Bergan the brigand who sees the Breen couple go by, and collapses with laughter at the story of the cryptic message.

"U.P." B spelled: "Up." Or perhaps it was only "U.P." It's never entirely clear what the letters in the anonymous note were.

Let's say U.P. for short, C said. It's may be a twisted idiom from *Oliver Twist*, and has a lot of possible interpretations.

The commonest or most vulgar is "You pee," A said. Or, "You pee with an erection," if we add the *up*.

I think he's pulling our leg, Professor Jones said in all seriousness. Let's get back to the chitchat in the chapter.

One half slander and the other of Erin, A said. From rumor to legend . . .

They both combine throughout "Cyclops," C said.

Joyce rebelled in a Rabelaisian way against this mean-mindedness of his fellow countrymen, said A, by providing a comic catalogue of them, examining them under a magnifying glass in the manner of Swift.

Yes, we know that while he was writing "Cyclops," Joyce reread Swift, C told us.

Speaking of Rabelaisian lists, A said, the list (using the word in its sartorial sense) with the most historical and mythical weight here is the one the Citizen is wearing, in its epic-parodic transposition.

The row of stones hanging from his belt, B recalled, on which are carved the figures of numerous heroes and historical characters.

The strangest thing, said C, is that this fervent nationalist adopts Velázquez and Shakespeare, for example, transformed into Patricio Velasquez and Patrick W. Shakespeare.

Thou art Patrick, and upon this rock I will build my English, A said.

Of course, the satire on Irish nationalism in "Cyclops" can be extrapolated to other nations, Professor Jones said.

It's the same the whole world over, A said. Worlds in words . . .

And Joyce parodies all of them, C said. From legal jargon to high society gossip to the journalistic language of the sports page.

Perhaps the funniest passages, said A, are the scraps or snatches of Gaelic, those touches of color or local dialect the Citizen uses to make his language purer.

Bi i dho husht! A ventriloquist's voice rang out.

What? asked A.

What did you say? we all asked at once.

Silence! exclaimed the voice. We all turned towards the man with the Macintosh.

ULYSSES II.12.doc

TITLE: The Cyclops

SETTING: Barney Kiernan's pub

TIME: 4:30–5:45 P.M.

SCIENCE, ART: Politics

SYMBOL: The Fenians

COLOR: Green

ORGAN: Muscles

TECHNIQUE: Gigantism, alternating asymmetry of two first-person narratives

MEANING: Egocidal terror

CORRESPONDENCES:
Cyclops: The Citizen
Noman: "I"
Ulysses' stake: Bloom's cigar

At the opening of "Cyclops," on a corner of Arbour Hill (probably at the intersection with Manor Street), a street that runs parallel to the north bank of the Liffey, in northwest Dublin, a chimney-sweep almost pokes out the eye of the unnamed narrator of this chapter with his brush, said the Cicerone, pointing with his wand,

and starting, by way of this collision, the allusion to the Cyclops Ulysses blinded with a stake.

Red-hot poker in the eye, A said.

The Cicerone continued:

Then this anonymous narrator by chance meets his friend Joe Hynes (the *Evening Telegraph* journalist who drew up the list of all those who attended Dignam's funeral), and the two of them go to Barney Kiernan's pub on Little Britain Street (this geographical enclave, the parish of Saint Michan, is described in the florid language of a nineteenth-century version of a Celtic saga) where the Citizen lords and laps it with his mongrel Garryowen. And to start off the genealogies of the tribe—really a tribe of savages—Hynes buys three pints of Guinness.

Professor Jones declared in ringing tones: Joyce identified the nameless narrator as Thersites, the deformed, sycophantic Greek to whose back and shoulders Ulysses applied his scepter in the second book of the *Iliad*. He also has something of the gossipy Thersites of Shakespeare's *Troilus and Cressida* about him, but in this exuberant chapter, as well as this transposed Thersites, and then the first Cyclops almost blinded by a Dublin chimneysweep, there is a second narrator who is far more slippery and cunning, a real no-man or Mr. Nobody who slides in everywhere, interpolates and questions, interrupting with his high-flown parodies (thirty-three altogether) the low language of the initial narrator.

Who is the *vox populi*, A said, the voice of the chattering people of Dublin. Everybody and nobody.

And the other one? asked B.

His Master's Voice, A said.

Tu quoque . . . B said, shaking his head disapprovingly.

Another questioning voice, A said. Did he mishear or just miss her?

Let the sweeper sweep . . . and Professor Jones swept over to the ring of people listening to the Cicerone, who was explaining that as Bloom goes into Kiernan's pub in search of the lawyer Martin Cunningham to offer him unselfish help in sorting out an insurance policy for Dignam's widow, as Bloom casts his codfish eyes over the pub and takes the risk of going in despite the growls from Garryowen, who is as anti-Semitic as his master and the anonymous narrator (We don't actually know about his master, interrupted A, because Garryowen's real owner is old man Giltrap, the maternal grandfather of Gerty MacDowell, a pretty young woman we will get a more rewarding view of in the next episode), as Bloom, that is, enters the pub, Hynes is reading a badly spelled letter from someone called H. Rumbold, a Master Barber from Liverpool, offering his services as a hangman to the High Sheriff of Dublin. In his curriculum vitae he writes of hanging Joe Gann and Toad Smith—but Professor Jones broke in again, not that he was being pedantic, to inform us that Joyce like Dante put his enemies into the Hades of *Ulysses*, such as the British ambassador in Switzerland, Horace Rumbold, as well as two employees at the British consulate in Zurich: Gann and Smith, who did not give him the help he thought he deserved in his legal battles against another of the consulate's employees, Henry Carr (who we find transformed into an army private in "Circe"), regarding an amateur English theater company in which the author of *Exiles* was then performing.

The Cicerone said:

"Cyclops" is full of references to violence: hangings, lynching, executions, corporal punishments, all of which contrast with Bloom's pacific, conciliatory nature. He always does things in moderation, so for example during the passage about the hangman and his past prowess he apologizes for not accepting Hynes's invitation to drink and so that the latter won't be offended asks instead for a twopenny cigar, which he waves about like a foul-smelling but inoffensive stake. And to continue showing how little he fits into this brutal, enclosed atmosphere, Bloom gives a scientific lecture to the group, transfigured into Herr Professor Luitpold Blumenduft (although it's not exactly the scent of flowers that comes from his cigar), explaining to them all in graphic detail and expression, *corpora cavernosa*, etc., why hanged man have erections.

It's not orchitis, A said, perhaps remembering Mr. Flower. But Garryowen is already gulping down the scraps from a tin of Jacob's biscuits, and the Citizen is lifting his elbow while he spouts his patriotic, xenophobic diatribes, interrupted by the parodies of the parodist or anonymous chronicler and the narrator's digressions, which leave no straw man standing—not even Bloom, whose supposed dirty linen he washes in public, including Mrs. Bloom's underwear, as if he has the royal seal of approval, poking his nose and other features as well into Bloom's private life, cornering him until he lets out a slip of the tongue: my wife's admirers, he says, instead of advisers; but the narrator had sniffed out from the start that the relations between Molly and Boylan go beyond the strictly professional, and that this very afternoon they had something else to do besides deciding on the program for

Molly's next concert . . . To such a dirty-minded narrator, virtues end up as defects, and in his chatter, he clucks on about Bloom's love of animals, pokes fun at his humanitarian impulses and amateur inventions, parodying the children's song about Liz the Black Hen, under whose backside Bloom softly puts his hand in search of a new treasure. Bloom soaks up the punishment, as if he were one of the boxers in the epic fight between the Irishman Keogh and Bennett the Englishman, parodied here in purest journalese. Bloom defends himself more vigorously when the anti-Semitic attacks begin. He declares—before making a declaration about universal love (life is love . . .)—that he is Irish as well as being Jewish. And that Mendelssohn, Marx, Mercadante, and Spinoza were also Jews . . . Although in the case of the Italian composer Mercadante (1795–1870), as Professor Jones quickly pointed out, Bloom was muddying the waters, since he appropriates him in much the same way that the Gaelic nationalists laid claim to Patrick Shakespeare. Yet Bloom is able to conclude, said the Cicerone, that "Christ was a jew like me," [sic], something he will not be pardoned for. But the brutal Citizen's attacks, as he lifts his pint of strong beer, are also directed against British "syphilisation," and he will not listen to the protests that it is no good adopting Nelson's tactics and turning a blind eye (the right one) to the telescope, and so not noticing the beam in his own, A insisted. The Cicerone said that once more Bloom has proven himself to be out of place in this cavern of macho males, once more the foreigner among his fellow countrymen. His broad vision contrasts with the cockeyed view of the Cyclops, Professor Jones pointed out. A new misunderstanding and a fresh piece of gossip makes Bloom the butt of their anger and scorn, the Cicerone explained: Lenehan arrives with the news that Throwaway won the Gold Cup, and suggests Bloom must have won a tidy sum with this victory. And then, the drop that makes the cup overflow: Bloom the Jew doesn't even pay for a round. While the narrator pisses out his beer, the Jew's winnings are magnified in his imagination, so that he rejects outright Bloom's claim that Ireland is his homeland too, telling himself in full flow: Impissible that my own Zion could ever be home to that fucking Bloomjew!

In the short time after Bloom leaves the pub to go and find Martin Cunningham in the courthouse, the attacks grow even more virulent. When Cunningham finally arrives at the pub asking for Bloom, Lenehan replies that he's off defrauding widows and orphans. People should be told. Fortunately Bloom soon returns and is able to leave the pub safe and sound with Cunningham. The Citizen Cyclops fails to hit his departing tilbury with the Jacob's biscuit tin he throws at it.

Another *throwaway*—Jacob for Elijah escaping in his chariot, A said.

Passageways

I

The chimneysweep with his brushes and ladders, said the Cicerone pointing with his wand, almost pokes the eye out of the cheerful narrator on the dangerous corner at the start of "Cyclops."

II

The description of the Citizen, magnified into an Irish hero, recreates the nineteenth-century recreations of the Celtic legends, said Professor Jones. It makes use of the gigantism of Rabelais's massive encyclopedic parodies, which establishes a parallel with the Cyclopean descriptions in Homer.

Imitates and dynamites such enormities, so many delusions of past grandeur, A said.

The Cicerone measured the most outstanding characteristics of the red-haired, freckly giant, whose eyes were as big as cauliflowers and whose nostrils were so deep a field-lark could have nested there. He reviewed the images of the mythical heroes and heroines of myth and literature immortalized in the carved stones he was bearing like a chastisement on his belt.

From Cuchulin and Conn of a hundred battles to Don Philip O'Sullivan Beare, by way of Velázquez, the Last of the Mohicans, and Captain Nemo.

Who was that Don Philip? asked A.

Don Philip O'Sullivan Beare (1590?–1660?), Professor Jones read on the Macintosh screen. A Spanish soldier and historian, born in Cork and author of *Historiae Catholicae Iberniae Compendium* (Lisbon, 1621).

The Cicerone poked his wand into the gorse bushes proliferating on the giant's mountainous knees. At his feet, the mongrel Garryowen dozed.

May the good "Patricio" Velázquez forgive us, but alongside him we are all minimal *Meninas* . . . said A.

III

The Cicerone pointed out:

Barney Kiernan's pub, near the courthouse, was a real museum of crime. It had fake coins pinned to the bar, and souvenirs and documents of criminals and hangmen on the walls. It seems the perfect place to recreate an execution (one of the most comic passages in the chapter, which demonstrates the hypocrisy of all the legal ceremony involved: a real theater of cruelty) and to list all of the hangman's equipment. The quartering knife, several bladed weapons for the bloody disemboweled victim, a pan to collect the entrails in, and two milkjugs to catch the blood.

IV

The Cicerone:

The rabid dog, red-eyed from thirst and hydrophobia dripping from his jaws, as fanatical as his master, terrifies Bloom. The Irish wolf dog setter Garryowen becomes the bard with the name of the mythical king Owen Garry, the true voice of his true master, the Citizen, with whom he sits at the bar and barks in Gaelic.

My friend the muttering mutt, said A.

V

The Cicerone:

Bloom the Jew asserts that Ireland is his nation. The Citizen spits and dries his mouth with a handkerchief that immediately becomes a medieval tapestry with intricate embroidery showing the four evangelists in each corner, each one with his symbol. Saint Matthew with a "bogoak sceptre," Ireland's saintly tree, Saint

Mark with a puma, nobler than the heraldic English lion, Saint Luke with a Kerry calf, and Saint John with a golden eagle from Carrantuohill, Ireland's highest mountain.

VI

Now we're coming to the chapter's apotheosis, said Professor Jones, gesturing as though about to throw something with his closed left fist. The part that corresponds to Ulysses and his companions' escape in their black ship, avoiding the rocks that, blinded with rage, the Cyclops Polyphemus hurls after them.

Seeing the pub crowd's growing hostility toward Bloom, Martin Cunningham and Jack Power hurry away with him and somebody called Crofton (a member of secret Protestant Orange Lodge, taken from the *Dubliners* story "Ivy Day in the Committee Room") in their Irish tilbury, said the Cicerone, poetically transformed into a Homeric vessel, and then, at the end, when the Citizen throws the empty biscuit tin and orders his dog to chase after him, into Elijah's chariot rising into the heavens. We see the scene through a Cyclopean eye that inflates the tilbury into a covered coach and ruins his aim.

Yes, it's said of the Citizen, "the sun was in his eyes," Professor Jones said. A slang expression meaning he was drunk.

13. NAUSICAA

The mist of a summer evening closed in on the hillocks, mounds, and distant promontories, while the last glow of the evening sun caressed the outline of lofty Howth, guardian of the bay and all its furtive loves, lingering on the rocks and dunes of Sandymount, settling gently on the facade of the Star of the Sea church in Sandymount Road, now a refuge for repentant drinkers raising their pleas to the Virgin—"Spiritual vessel, pray for us, honourable vessel . . ."—and lighting up the horizon for a dreamy young woman who sat staring into the distance on the rocks of Sandymount beach, enjoying the sunset and the cool breeze with her friends Cissy Caffrey and Edy Boardman. They were looking after Edy's little brother, Bobby, a baby aged eleven months and nine days in his "pushcar," as well as two twins aged four: Tommy and Jacky Caffrey, curly-haired and in their sailor suits, making

Martello sandcastles on the beach and then becoming little Marses unto themselves, mischievous gods of war.

Cissy Caffrey was no sissy, almost a tomboy, although she was clever and funny, like when she painted on a moustache in burnt cork and went out into the street wearing her father's suit and hat, it was hilarious, or when she took it into her head to paint men's faces on her fingernails in red ink . . . and her Moorish eyes and cherry-ripe red lips were always sincere when she smiled . . . although the high-heeled shoes she insisted on wearing made her legs look even longer and skinnier. Edy Boardman was shorter than Cissy, and had something of the confirmed spinster about her, with her glasses and shortsighted slightly squinting eyes; sometimes rather jealous of her friend. But no description could do justice to the dreamy young woman sitting next to them. Gerty MacDowell was her name, and she had no reason to be jealous of anyone, although she was more a Giltrap than a MacDowell, as she had inherited the exuberance of her maternal line. She was slender and reedlike, graciously fragile, with a languid pride about her and a natural refinement emphasized by her marvelous ivory complexion, and delicate hands which we will never tire of praising, cared for with lemon juice and Larola, the queen of creams. Her pious pallor and female frailty, due in part perhaps to one of those reversals particular to her sex and age, were becoming less noticeable now thanks to a new restorative that was more effective than Widow Welch's pills for women's problems, and helped bring out the fullness of her Cupid's-bow, rosebud lips, Hellenic in their perfection. But really where the whole splendor of Irish enchantment shone through was in Gerty's blue starry eyes, her captivating eyes of the purest Irish blue, her shiny eyelashes, framed by well-defined black eyebrows—silkily seductive thanks to the advice of Madame Vera Verity in the *Princess's Novelettes* weekly, who also helped her overcome her habit of blushing. And while pausing for a moment to admire the rose-petal blush that so delicately tinged Gerty's smooth cheeks, we decide to save her crowning, abundant glory for later—let her show it off to the mysterious gentleman in black she will come to see admiring her on the evening beach, shortly after losing herself in romantic dreams of marriage to her ideal man: "Art thou real, my ideal?" Her ideal would have to be very different from her father, who was so violent because of his weakness for drink, despite which of course she loved and respected him. Why, could Gerty MacDowell's father be the anonymous and irascible Citizen of the previous chapter? A question we will leave hanging in the air. Gerty would naturally make an ideal wife for her ideal husband, who would have to be tall and broad-shouldered, a manly man, someone she could take care of and spoil—he should have everything he wants at home, Gerty's a dab hand in the kitchen, and their home sweet home would have to be very cozy indeed, with a drawing room decorated with engravings and pictures and a photograph of Grandfather's lovely dog Garryowen, so clever and human it was, as if he were talking rather than barking . . .

Although modest, Gerty was dressed in the latest fashion. She herself had dyed her blouse electric blue with Dolly dyes. Her blouse had a V-neck that dipped into the valley of her cleavage and a handkerchief pocket she used instead for a piece of cotton wool doused in perfume. This blouse matched a three-quarter length navy-blue skirt that highlighted the blue of Gerty's eyes and set off her figure to perfection. Her black straw hat decorated with a blue ribbon and a bow of the same color added a coquettish touch.

Her fashionable shoes, with patent leather toe caps and a buckle on the instep, helped show off her well-turned ankles and her shapely legs encased in a pair of fine, transparent stockings. Her underwear on this seashore evening was blue, her favorite color.

Gerty was lost in her daydreams, lulled by the organ music from the nearby church, when Jacky Caffrey almost lost his ball by throwing it toward the seaweed-covered rocks—but fortunately a gentleman in black who happened to be there was able to rescue it. The gentleman energetically threw the ball back toward Cissy Caffrey, but the spherical projectile rolled down a slope and came to rest right underneath Gerty's skirt. It had found its target. The twins shouted for the ball, and Cissy said she should kick it as far as possible. As Gerty was no footballer, however, she missed it completely on her first attempt ("If you fail try again," Edy Boardman says, jealous because well aware who the gentleman opposite is staring at), but, determined not to fail, she raised her skirt a little and this time kicked the ball a good distance. Protected by the brim of her hat and by the evening mist, Gerty was bold enough then to take a look at the man. His face seemed to her the saddest she had ever seen. Yes, it was her he was looking at, and his eyes burned in her like the incense and candles in the nearby church. From his dark eyes and pallid face, Gerty concluded he was a foreigner. He was wearing strict mourning, and grief marked his features. "Refuge of sinners. Comfortress of the afflicted. *Ora pro nobis*," came the litany from the Star of the Sea. The twins again went perilously close to the sea, while Gerty realized the stranger was admiring her transparent stockings. She took off her hat for a moment to smooth her hair and a cascade of nut-brown waves spilled down around her shoulders, a fleeting radiant vision. She could see the glint of admiration in the man's eyes, and this set her trembling. She wished they could be alone together on the beach: it was high time the children went home. Then Cissy went boldly up to the stranger to ask him the time. He put his hand in his pocket, raised his watch to his ear, and said he was sorry but it had stopped. It was getting late; a bat flew hither and thither across the velvet twilight, and the lights from the picturesque lighthouses swept round the bay. A prelude to the explosions of light—green, blue, and purple—about to light up the night sky: the fireworks from the Mirus charity bazaar opened a few hours earlier by the Viceroy. They will all run to admire them in the west, beyond the houses and the church. All except for Gerty and the stranger, that is: they each stayed where they were, alone at last, piercing each other with their eyes. Her breath was bated—he was a master bater. The trembling of his hands and face was continued in the quiver of her cheek. She leaned back to look at the shower of colors high in the sky, cupping one knee in her hands, and as he was the only one there to see, offered him the sight of her legs, her blue garters and white nainsook knickers, while something dark and soft slid across the lake of the sky, O! she trembled in all her limbs from leaning so far back, O! the blinding flash and a cascade of stars and dew gushed out and melted in the gray air around the man in black outlined against the rock. Now the man seemed motionless and silent to the girl, who had shared her secret with the little bat flying hither and thither, but bats don't see or speak.

Gerty! Gerty! Sharp cries called and recalled her. She made the generous gesture of leaving the man her scrap of cotton wool as a memento before standing up. By now it was really dark, as with the dignity of a queen she walked off along the beach, taking care where she put her feet because there was seaweed and stones and bits of wood on the sand, walking carefully and slowly because, as Leopold Bloom—our romantic lead in his mourning black—then discovered, she was—carefully now—tight boots? slowly—another piece of wood? she was . . . "She's lame! O!"

The first part of "Nausicaa," C said, until Bloom has finished masturbating and starts his monologue, is a parody of romantic novels, of advice columns in women's magazines, and of the language used in adverts for female beauty products . . .

Whereas "Cyclops" presented a series of harsh stereotypes of machismo, A said, "Nausicaa" is a showcase of chic clichés about femininity.

Well, Joyce himself provided a perfect summary of the chapter in a letter to his friend, the painter Frank Budgen, said Professor Jones, opening his notebook: "*Nausicaa* is written in a namby-pamby jammy marmalady drawersy (alto là!) style with effects of incense, mariolatry, masturbation, stewed cockles, painter's palette, chitchat, circumlocutions, etc., etc."

Bloom's realist monologue forms a counterpoint to Gerty's dated idealism. His feet are on the ground.

And his hand on the wet patch on his shirt, said A.

But Gerty is not as much in the clouds as you think, B said. She knows very well what she's doing and what the mysterious man on the beach is doing too.

As well as being a Peeping Tom, Bloom also has great powers of observation, A said. On the beach he recalls how he knew perfectly well that the newspaper boys were making fun of him when he left the *Freeman* in "Aeolus."

And the virgin Gerty is not especially spotless, B said. She knows what it means to masturbate. The sexual relationship between her and Bloom may not be perfect, but in the end it is the only one Bloom has all day.

He tells himself in a very matter-of-fact way that it was a good thing he did not do it in the bath, C said. And even more sensibly, since there is nothing he can do about it, he hopes that perhaps Boylan has given his wife some money during his visit.

But Molly's adultery still affects him, A said. And he notes that his watch stopped at exactly half past four in the afternoon.

Bloom spends about two hours in Dignam's widow's house, from six to eight, the Cicerone calculated, before coming to Sandymount beach to enjoy the view.

And the smell, A said, because he sniffs the cheap rose perfume on Gerty's piece of cotton wool, and thinks of the one Molly uses.

Opoponax! B exclaimed. And at the opening of his waistcoat he also smells the lemon scent of his cake of soap.

Smell and sight are the two senses that do all the work in this chapter, A said.

Especially sight, A said, and not just because of Bloom's voyeurism and Gerty's exhibitionism. The chapter is very pictorial.

The Cicerone waved his wand and said:

We can draw a parallel with Stephen, who wrote a poem that morning on this same beach—Bloom now uses his stick to write an enigmatic message in the sand. Perhaps he doesn't finish it: I. AM. A.

Perhaps he means I AM ALPHA, said Professor Jones. Or perhaps simply A.M.A, *Anima Mundi Anno.*

By an extraordinary chance, Bloom's "wooden pen" gets stuck in the sand when he flings it away, B said. Perhaps that completes the hieroglyph.

The Masters often wrote incomprehensible messages upon the earth, A said.

The Cicerone said:

But Bloom rubs out the message with his boot. (Ah, no Master he, said A.) Feeling sleepy, he dozes off, lulled by a sea of sensual images, a mixture of Gerty's girdle, phrases from his letter to Martha Clifford and from *The Sweets of Sin*, and "Spanish" Molly's generous curves, when all at once the cuckoo clock in the priest's house at 3 Leahy Terrace, opposite the Star of the Sea church, strikes nine o'clock.

Cuckoo, A imitated. Has the man with the Macintosh dozed off as well?

ULYSSES II.13.doc

TITLE: Nausicaa

SETTING: Rocks on Sandymount beach

TIME: 8:00–9:00 P.M.

SCIENCE, ART: Painting

SYMBOL: Virgin

COLOR: Gray, blue

ORGAN: Eye, mouth

TECHNIQUE: Tumescence (sugary third-person narrative), detumescence (descending monologue)

MEANING: The projected mirage

CORRESPONDENCES:
Phaeacia: Star of the Sea church
Nausicaa: Gerty

Cuckoo, A trilled again. Or *cuckold*. The cuckoo clock launches its nine cuckoos like nine accusations of the fact that Bloom has been cuckolded, while a bat glides gently through the air, like Bloom's own memories, flowing in a daydream that is a foretaste of another novel, of the flow of words of the washerwomen at the end of the "Anna Livia" section of *Finnegans Wake*, doing their washing as the bats fly round their heads.

Passageways

I

An idealized portrayal of Nausicaa and her friends on the beach at Sandymount, said A. They are very close before the ball games begin. But the game is a real battle.

II

Gerty kicks off ceremoniously, A commented. The kickoff for the *beau ténébreux*, the melancholic Hebrew, the mysterious stranger in black opposite them who cannot take his eyes off her, second time lucky, don't give up, and Gerty with her beautiful stockings scores a bull's-eye . . .

III

The Cicerone said:

The art of this chapter is painting. "Nausicaa" is full of landscapes and pictorial descriptions. Gerty's thoughts are expressed in paintings like those she wants to hang in the drawing room of her ideal home. As Gerty stares out to sea, the landscape itself becomes a cliché: the seascape she once saw a pavement artist draw in colored chalks. It is very appropriate that it's this kind of "painter" who represents the art of painting in "Nausicaa."

IV

The bat crisscrosses the sky while Gerty is stirred by the sight of the summer twilight, A said, crossed by the lights of the lighthouses she would like to copy in paint and which also anticipate the illumination and gushing pleasure the fireworks are going to give Bloom: the rocket, the Roman candle, and the flare which are about to explode O! and flood the sky, gently melting. Soft, soft, as Stephen softly said that morning on this same spot. Gentle.

The bat represents Bloom's own ambivalent world, said Professor Jones. A bird and mouse combined.

You think so? asked B, raising her eyes to make two circumflex accents. At any rate, Bloom describes the bat very kindly: like a little man in a cloak with little hands.

The time Gerty sees the bat and the lights from the lighthouses must be about half past eight, calculated Professor Jones. Sunset in Dublin that day was at 8:27 P.M.

V

At last they are alone, A said, with the bat the only witness to their distant love. Gerty sees the mysterious man's hand shaking at the precious moment she too begins to quiver along with the bursting sky, and as the Roman candle rises and rises she leans still further back to give to him alone the spectacle of her immodest modesty.

14. THE OXEN OF THE SUN

Mrs. Purefoy's childbirth at the National Maternity Hospital in Holles Street is a dystocia, or truly difficult labor. Almost as difficult as this chapter, said the Cicerone in the doorway to this white room of the House. It cost Joyce more than a thousand hours of enormous effort. *Deshil Holles Eamus*, he intoned with thunderous voice, *Deshil Holles Eamus*, thundered three times, *Deshil Holles Eamos*, and we followed him in, while Professor Jones explained that this incantation in dog Gaelic-Latin means "Let's head south, to Holles Street"; that is, to the Maternity Hospital.

TITLE: The Oxen of the Sun	ORGAN: Womb
SETTING: The hospital at 29–31 Holles Street	TECHNIQUE: Embryonic development
TIME: 10:00–11:00 P.M.	MEANING: The eternal herds
SCIENCE, ART: Medicine	CORRESPONDENCES:
	Thrinacia (island of the god Helios): The Hospital
SYMBOL: Mothers	Lampetia, Phaetusa (daughters of Helios): Nurses Callan and Quigley
COLOR: White	Helios: Dr. Horne
	Oxen: Fertility
	Crime (killing the oxen): Fraud

There follows another three-part invocation, this time to Helios, the fecundating Sun God, which through the repeated phallic exclamation *Horhorn* is linked to Dr. Andrew D. Horne, one of the directors of the maternity hospital. If we take the *Horhorn* by the horns, it could also relate to Blazes Boylan, if we remember what Lenehan told him in the Sirens' bar (see p. 158). And the set of three threes closes with a midwife's triple exclamation that the newborn is a boy: *hoopsa boyaboy.* "Boy" sounds like the word for "ox" in Portuguese, A interjected buoyantly, joining in the banter. Boy oh boy! Professor Jones echoed her, concluding that the entire chapter is contained in embryonic form in those three opening incantations: the first directing us to the Hospital, where "father" and "son"—Bloom and Stephen—finally meet up, and likewise standing in for the language soup that existed prior to the birth of English, with rudiments of Latin (*Eamos*), Gaelic (*Deshil*), and Anglo-Saxon (*Holles*), all of which will fuse and develop over the various stages of the growth of the English language; the second introducing the theme of fecundation, which is treated with great fecundity throughout the chapter; and the third, finally, announcing the birth of Mrs. Mina Purefoy's son. Let's not get ahead of ourselves, said the Cicerone, but Professor Jones sneaked in mention of the fact that the mother-to-be had been fortunately endowed with the name of the most famous Dublin obstetrician of the time, Richard Dancer Purefoy.

After his moment of release on Sandymount beach, Bloom arrives at Holles Street Hospital to find out what has happened to Mina Purefoy, who has been in labor for three days, as Josie Breen informed him in "Laestrygonians." He is met at the door by Nurse Callan, who had been his landlady nine years earlier, when he lived with Molly and Milly in Holles Street. As the door opens, the night sky is rent by a flash of lightning, reminding us of the storm that broke over Ulysses and his companions as a punishment for killing Helios's oxen. Shortly afterward, to complete the allusions to fecundity, rain starts to fall. Nurse Callan (she is called a "nun," Professor Jones explained, because the word *nurse* came into the English language from French, and here we are still at an earlier stage of the language, i.e. Anglo-Saxon, which had the word *nun* from Latin) sees that Bloom was in mourning, and their conversation turns to a grave consideration of the cycle of life, paraphrasing the Book of Job in archaic English (in essence: man came naked into the world and will leave it naked). But life follows death, and Nurse Callan tells Bloom that, although Mrs. Purefoy's labor is the most difficult she's ever been present at, it will not be long now before the baby is born.

The junior Doctor Dixon comes out from a noisy room nearby. Dixon once treated Bloom for a bee-sting at the Mater Misericordiae Hospital on Eccles Street (in Medieval English, the bee-sting becomes inflated to a dragon wound), and invites Bloom to join the party going on in the room on the ground floor of the hospital. Dixon has been spending time there with the medical students Lynch, Madden, Crotthers, and "Punch" Costello (Buck Mulligan arrives later on with another student, Alec Bannon), as well as the sportswriter Lenehan, and Stephen Dedalus, already the worse for wear from drink.

Bloom feels obliged to accept a pint of beer (here called mead) but after taking only a sip he surreptitiously pours it into his neighbor's glass. Nurse Quigley asks them to make less noise, and from the floor above they hear the screams of the mother giving birth.

Professor Jones maintained that Mrs. Purefoy's giving birth also represents a literary birth, and in particular Joyce himself delivering himself of his novel after the long and painful gestation of *Ulysses*. The Professor recalled that Stephen launches a homily in which, willy-nilly, he presents the beginning and end of a writer: through his spirit, mortal flesh becomes undying word.

The word is made parodic flesh in this chapter, A said. And every parody gives birth to or aborts a rhetorical flourish.

The battle of styles and parodies, Professor Jones argued—forty of them altogether—in the end leads, in a flash of lightning, to the birth of a new life, purified by art: a new Purefoy.

Nothing but sterile lies! A exclaimed. Every new style attempts to reproduce life but in the end kills it and puts the artifice of art in its place. You think you're getting a birth, but then they pull a fast one, and you're left not with Purefoy but purest Joyce . . .

In fact, the parodies sometimes seem like coitus interruptus, interrupting the story of the chapter, C said.

And you're interrupting our discussion of the hospital with your theorizing, said B. Let the Cicerone continue.

While upstairs Mrs. Purefoy is struggling with her pain, downstairs the men are in a life-and-death debate about those extreme cases when a choice has to be made between saving the life of a mother-to-be or that of her child—they all shout in favor of the mother.

Libations and deliberations continue to flow, laced with giggles and guffaws, producing variations on the themes of conception and contraception, some of which turn into blasphemy, as in the *jeu d'esprit* about the Holy Spirit-Pigeon, who according to *La vie de Jésus* by Léo Taxil, already mentioned in "Proteus," was the one who put the Virgin Mary in her embarrassing situation. Mention is also made of other strange birds, such as the whore known as Bird-in-the-Hand. This crude student talk, full of sexual allusions, contrasts with Bloom's attitude—once again he seems out of place, with his respect for maternity and the cycle of life and nature. By means of a series of literary pastiches (as many as there are weeks in a pregnancy) that move from ancient Anglo-Saxon to the many different kinds of North American slang at the start of the twentieth century, passing through Mandeville, Malory, Milton, Bunyan, Nashe, Swift, Sterne, Dickens, and Carlyle, among others, Joyce presents the embryonic development of the English language. The word becomes flesh in the new Purefoy. In addition to presenting a summary of the evolution of the English language, the nine parts of the chapter follow the growth of a fetus and the evolution of animals on earth, as well as incorporating elements from earlier chapters of *Ulysses*. In a much-quoted letter, Joyce referred to the allegorical conception of this chapter, in which "Bloom is the spermatozoon, the hospital the womb, the nurse the ovum, Stephen the embryo." He also pointed out that his basic idea is "the crime committed against fecundity by sterilizing the act of coition."

Joyce's views on this subject were not very "uterodox," said A. In spite of Stephen's blasphemy against the Virgin, his position is not very far from that of the Catholic Church. We know for example that he got lippy in the *brasserie* Lipp, successfully convincing one of his friend Paul Léon's nieces not to have an abortion.

I also think that we may find in this chapter the embodiment of the ghost of the third child Joyce never had, said B. When Nora had an abortion in Trieste early in August, 1908, Joyce was the most affected. He looked on the three-month-old fetus with affection and no small curiosity.

The rudiments of Rudy . . . A said.

There is a lot to be said about Joyce's concept of conception and the cult of fatherhood, C said. Above all, about his extraordinary love of the family. Though in this chapter he seems to be criticizing in equal measure three extremes: sex without creation, creation without sex (the Virgin), and creation without love, represented by the beastly Buck Mulligan.

That's right, the Cicerone said. Mr. Malachi Mulligan, who arrives at the Hospital accompanied by Alec Bannon, begins to hand around a joke business card in which he's styled himself "Fertiliser and Incubator. Lambay Island," rich in marine birds' eggs, from which place he offers his services free of charge as a *fecundator* of any female of whatever condition or class.

With Mulligan's arrival, the jokes and drinks flow even more freely. Sexual allusions flood the episode, particularly with regard to sartorial "protection," to keep out the rain, such as hoods, macs, and all different sorts of rubbers, umbrella-diaphragms, etc. There is much recourse to French words, for the greater glory of French letters . . .

At this point, A said, it is relevant to remember the hand-play, or onanistic piece introduced by Mulligan in the "Scylla and Charybdis" episode, subtitled, "A Honeymoon in the Hand."

We should also remember, said B, that Bloom visits the hospital after he has masturbated. His morality, if it can be called that, and his rejection of the students' position in favor of contraception, is hypocritical to say the least. Not to mention the fact that for years he has not fulfilled his duties as a husband, pardon my French, and has purely epistolary relationships that are all hot air.

Let he who is without sin cast the first theater piece, as dramatist Mulligan might say, A said. Bloom's sins are venereal, that is venial.

He who is without a skin, laughed B. When Joyce describes Mulligan and Bannon's drenched clothes after their journey from Mullingar, he brings in another item of clothing and another relationship: that of Milly Bloom, whom Bannon is courting and for whom he is thinking of buying a cloak . . .

Now we've reached Sterne, steering us back toward laughter, hysterically enough, said A.

One of the best parodies in the entire chapter, C said.

(A parenthesis, Professor Jones insisted, to give an example of the gradual, sly, and tightly controlled way that Joyce supplies us with information in *Ulysses*. In this novel, revelations always come little by little. At the end of the first chapter we are told in an ambiguous way that somebody called Bannon met in the county of Westmeath a pretty "photo girl." In the fourth chapter, we learn that this is Milly, Bloom's daughter, who works for a photographer in Mullingar. In this fourteenth chapter, we finally meet Bannon and hear his saucy comments about Milly. *Mille compléments*, A complemented.)

Shortly afterwards, the Cicerone pointed out, Dixon is called by Nurse Callan to help Mrs. Purefoy. The news that she has given birth to a son is received with great satisfaction and relief by Bloom. This is followed by a series of parodies and daydreams. We see, from Lynch's point of view, the scene of the blushing girl (her name was Sarah) and the young man (Lynch himself) who Father Conmee saw coming out of a hedge in "Wandering Rocks." The noise and loud conversations return, increasingly chaotic. While Stephen wallows in remorse with images of his dead mother, Bloom superimposes the image of his dead son Rudy on his memories of Stephen as a boy, and this revives his desire to be a father.

There is another peal of thunder, and Stephen (who is as terrified as was Joyce of storms) shouts "Burke's!," the pub round the corner in Denzille (now Fenian) Street, at the corner of Holles.

The racket continues in the bar, and Stephen is still paying for everyone's drinks. They all choose absinthe, except for Bloom, who orders a glass of wine.

The man in the brown macintosh makes another mysterious appearance. Bantam Lyons joins them, perhaps to give us eleven apostles, as it will soon be 11:00 P.M., time to close.

To continue the evolution of English prose, A said, it is noteworthy that at this time and in the bar, the barbarous bibulous boys break down into an English that recalls the nighttime dialect of *Finnegans Wake*.

"Shut your obstropolos," said B. Quiet your claptrap.

We ran, and the Cicerone waved his wand. The group breaks up (or did he say out?), Stephen and Lynch heading drunkenly for the red-light district of the next chapter. Bloom struggles after them, because he does not want the son of his friend Simon Dedalus—his own new prospective son—to come to any harm.

Hoopsa boyaboy hoopsa! A coughed like a calf.

Passageways

I

Bloom *ante portam,* A said. About to penetrate Maternity.

Hat in hand, said Professor Jones, to emphasize the symbolism of penetration.

The nurse or *sister* Callan opens the hospital door wide, and Bloom thinks that although she is beautiful she has no children, and her womb has not known the sweet pain of giving birth.

Yes, she has not known the "joys" Mrs. Purefoy is experiencing, said B: giving birth to her ninth child, after her twelfth pregnancy.

II

In the style of Sir John Mandeville, a fourteenth-century English knight known for his *Travels*, we have a description of the birch-wood table from Finland supported by four Finnish dwarves where the merry hospital drinkers sit. On the table are the "frightful swords and knives" that are their cut-rate cutlery, marvelous enchanted bubbles that are actually bottles of beer, and a shiny silver platter containing headless fish floating in an oily water that turns out to be nothing less than a tin of sardines in oil.

III

Though we haven't quite reached Joyce's parody of Sterne's *Tristram Shandy*, A said, we soon come to a "cock and bull story" nonetheless, or in any case, the parable of the English bull grazing in a field of clover. Following the papal bull that gave special dispensation to dispose of all that good Irish grass, Lord Harry's garlanded bull came to graze there. He was one who knew how green was his valley.

A sign planted in the grass read: "By the Lord Harry, Green is the grass that grows on the ground," B said.

Lord Harry is Henry II of England, and then Henry VIII, C said. Eventually, of course, he becomes John Bull himself.

IV

In a parody of the Gothic novel, Haines makes a terrifying appearance carrying a bundle of Celtic literature in one hand and a phial of laudanum in the other. "The black panther!" he cries, and vanishes.

V

Leopold Bloom ruminates on reminiscences and casts his mind back, mirrors within mirrors, across the span of his life. The wise advertisement canvasser sees himself as younger and younger: virile young man, lively young schoolboy, young child. Year after year is rolled back until the concave mirror goes hazy, and Bloom is nothing more than the seed of his father, in the distant past.

VI

The Cicerone pointed out:

Bloom has been staring at the scarlet label of a Number One Bass beer bottle for four minutes.

It's the favorite drink in this chapter, B said, even though it is English.

The triangle of the label, distorted in a more or less sub-cubist way in Bloom's meandering thoughts, becomes the triangular island Thrinacia (Sicily), where Bloom perhaps managed to write *I AM ALPHA* in the sand, said Professor Jones.

O megatherium! A said. It would be easier to see in that bottle the genius of the "island of terrible thirst": Hibernia . . .

Professor Jones took up the thread:

In Bloom's imaginings, the scarlet triangle of the bottle of Bass becomes confused with the adored image of his virginal daughter, Milly, that divine treasure of youth among the Pleiades, whose bejeweled veil became a delta, or the ruby triangle shining on the forehead of Taurus . . .

Bass-relief, A said with a sigh. A little relief down below, you know. Or do I mean release . . .

VII

Up and down. After copulation, contrition? A wondered.

For God's sake don't say that, Professor Jones protested. You have to believe that the aim of copulation is procreation. The act is a pact that concludes in birth. In moving Dickensian prose we are told that thanks to "the skill and patience of the physician" and Mina Purefoy's spirited battle, we are able to reach a happy *accouchement.*

All that's left is to cut the cord, A observed.

A new Purefoy makes his entrance into the world, Professor Jones droned on. He will be baptized with the names Mortimer Edward, after the third cousin of the father and accountant Theodore Purefoy: *that* Mortimer Edward has an influential position in the Treasury.

Mina Purefoy's fertile womb will be the sacrificial altar for the black mass celebrated in the next chapter, C said. The womb of Catholic Ireland: pure faith.

Par foi! exclaimed Professor Jones. On my faith . . .

VIII

Time. Closing time at Burke's. The Cicerone raised his wand toward the clock. Next to Stephen, the mysterious man in the macintosh reappears. In a parody of Westerns, he is called "Walking Mackintosh of lonely canyon."

Someone also calls him "Bartle the Bread," Professor Jones said. As if he was on the breadline. Remember that in "Wandering Rocks" we saw him eating a crust.

Man does not live by bread alone, A said. Perhaps that's why Stephen hasn't eaten in so long.

And he drinks enough for two, said Professor Jones. Here the man in the macintosh is apparently drinking Bovril, perhaps to end the chapter with another bovine allusion.

"Walking Mackintosh of lonely canyon," A drawled. Let's cut the crap.

15. CIRCE

City lights at night, or *nighttown*, the Cicerone said, the dim lights of street lamps and squalid houses with their front doors open. We're entering the red-light district along Mabbot (now James Joyce) Street, in the northeast of Dublin, not far from the wharves on the north bank of the Liffey. We're following Stephen and Lynch, who are headed for Bella Cohen's house, at 82 Tyrone (now Railway) Street.

Out of the night loom whores like bats with ragged shawls, Lilliputian dwarves, a deaf and dumb idiot who dribbles and has Saint Vitus's dance, filthy figures rummaging through the garbage, a bandy-legged little boy, a drunken navvy, two English soldiers, Compton and Carr, who laugh at Stephen all dressed in black ("Way for the parson"), an old bawd offering her wares. Then the characters from "Nausicaa" appear or reappear phantomlike: Edy Boardman boasting of putting one over on a rival; Cissy Caffrey, singing bawdy songs in the darkness; and her two little brothers too, the twins Tommy and Jacky, who climb a lamppost, which soon afterward the drunken navvy walks off with, carrying it over his shoulder.

After sending out a stream of snot, pressing against one nostril and blowing through the other, A specified.

The sordid and the poetic go hand in hand, B said. By the light of a candle stuck in a bottle, a grimy woman is combing the hair of a scrofulous child, then the blood-red uniforms of the soldiers glow in the light from a street lamp.

The whole chapter is full of fires and the play of will-o'-the-wisps, which are much more than wisps of fire, A said. Dramatic effects.

It's bathed in an expressionist light, C said.

Gaslight, candlelight, hallucinatory light, Professor Jones listed. Bloom and Stephen's hallucinations alternate with real events in the external world.

The hallucinations and visions of this chapter don't spring so much from the overheated imaginations of Stephen and Bloom (who isn't even drunk) as they leap from the page itself, C said. Words are the real hallucinogens here. Just as in its immediate precursor, Flaubert's *Temptation of Saint Anthony*, the visions come from reading, they rise directly from the book.

From the book of books, Professor Jones said, which *Ulysses* also is, in the encyclopedic-parodic manner of *Don Quixote*. This "Circe" is a rereading and rewriting of Flaubert's *Temptation of Saint Anthony* and Goethe's *Faust*, both written in dramatic form, not to mention those ghost-plays by Shakespeare, Ibsen, Strindberg, and Hauptmann, as well as Dante's *Inferno*, and even *Venus in Furs* by Sacher-Masoch and *Psychopathia Sexualis* by Krafft-Ebing.

Yes, but above all *Ulysses* reads itself, C said. Like *Hamlet*, it advances by reading the book of itself.

The *délire de lire*, A said. There's an avalanche of visions, illusions, and allusions here. It's so powerful we are the ones who fall prey to hallucinations due to this riot of rampant, outrageous images . . .

Images and words that dance and communicate with each other, C said, in a huge network of intertwining themes that defy all verisimilitude. The text has a truth that is independent of any naturalistic convention. That's why those who claim that even this chapter respects those conventions cannot understand how, for example, Stephen's mother uses words from Martha Clifford's letter, or how Bloom can repeat a spell Stephen read in the second-hand book he bought that afternoon.

Nebrakada femininum, B said. The complete spell in cod Arabic-Spanish is: *Se el yilo nebrakada femininum*. Little heaven of blessed femininity . . .

"Circe" is a recapitulation of the entire novel, C said. It's a crazy rereading of *Ulysses* itself. The novel's primary themes reappear distorted, as though they were in a hall of mirrors.

Like those Bloom looks at himself in at the start of the chapter, B said.

The intrusion of the real world into the fantasy world of the mind produces mental torments, Professor Jones commented. The brain waves ripple out like those caused by a pebble skimming the surface of a lake. Sometimes all it takes is a real sound, contact with some object, to set off the reverberation, the aural and visual illusions.

Proof enough is the button that pops from Bloom's back trouser pocket, B said. That breaks the spell.

"Bip!" A mimicked. And Bloom recovers his lost masculinity.

Or the cake of soap Bloom feels in his pocket, B went on, which immediately starts to shine like a solar disc, or medallion, in the center of which shines the freckly face of Sweny the druggist.

The midnight sun and the host, Professor Jones said. In *Finnegans Wake* it has become the rising sun and has a new lodger, Persse O'Reilly, in a parody of a Pears soap ad.

To free himself from Circe's enchantment, B said, the swine Stephen could do with some of Bloom's soap.

The soap and his mother's potato-talisman, C observed, are for Bloom the equivalent of the magic "moly" plant that protected Ulysses from Circe's charms. And of course, the all-powerful Molly also protects this impotent man . . .

His ejaculation in honor of Gerty on the beach was his best preservative. That's how Bloom avoids falling for the prostitutes' charms.

Bloom is a passive Saint Anthony, Professor Jones said. Whereas Stephen is an active Faust. But Joyce himself pointed out that the moly plant in this chapter has many leaves, two of the most important of which are imagination and laughter.

Fantasy is the opiate producing the visions in this chapter, A said, and its heroin(e).

Rather than in drug- or alcohol-induced visions, we need to think of a kaleidoscope and the way that some of the novel's themes recombine in new shapes, C said.

New visions or dreams, said A, in the dubious light of a dubious location.

Light is of great symbolic importance in this chapter, Professor Jones said. The opening is full of special optical effects. Some kids ask the deaf-mute an absurd question: "Where's the great light?" This is the light that Stephen, the Prince of Darkness, tries to knock out at the end of the chapter—with his ashplant.

Light and Luciferian fierceness, A exclaimed. While the shadowy pastor Stephen intones the *introit*, we enter into "Circe," though without abandoning all hope.

As the Cicerone entered the violet room, he raised his magic wand toward the bright words on the glowing screen.

ULYSSES II.15.doc

TITLE: Circe

SETTING: "Monto"—the red-light district and Bella Cohen's brothel

TIME: 11:25 P.M.–12:40 A.M.

SCIENCE, ART: Magic

SYMBOL: Whore

COLOR: Violet

ORGAN: Locomotive apparatus

TECHNIQUE: Hallucination

MEANING: The anthropophagic orca

CORRESPONDENCES:
Circe: Bella

Bloom is searching for the prodigal son, A declared. Lost? Following Stephen's sinful steps, he walks from Amiens Street Station to nighttown, or "Monto" as Dubliners used to call the area, after Montgomery Street, one of the most notorious in the city. Nowadays it's called Foley Street, Professor Jones informed us. Whereas once it was the full "Monty" . . . said A. This shady area isn't a shadow now on what it once was, when it had a reputation as the worst slum in Europe . . .

Now Bloom appears beneath the railway bridge on Talbot Street, the Cicerone said. He stops a moment outside number 64 to look at his distorted image in the concave and convex mirrors in Gillen the hairdresser's. Then, after deciding against fish and chips at Antonio Rabaiotti's shop at number 65, he goes into Olhausen's butcher shop at number 72, where he buys a still warm pig's trotter and a cold leg of lamb.

Feet are very important in this chapter, said Professor Jones. Bloom no longer has a leg to stand on, said A. A short time later he gives the meat to a dog. A dog as protean as the one in "Proteus," C said. Bloom is getting ready for the visions to come, A said, laying in a stock of new provisions. Shortly before he had already confirmed he had some bread and chocolate in his jacket pocket, B said. A cake of Fry's chocolate. Later he gives it to a prostitute, who then breaks off a bite to give back to him. He wonders if chocolate is an aphrodisiac.

First a group of cyclists, and then a tram cleaning the rails almost run him over, the Cicerone said. Luckily Bloom is carrying his mother's talisman, the potato of fortune, A said. A potato, soap, and *The Sweets of Sin* make up the stock of fetishes in his pockets, Professor Jones reminded us.

The visions begin when he turns the corner into Mabbot Street, the Cicerone said. First he sees a sinister Spanish figure wearing a broad-brimmed hat leaning against a tea and wine shop (*"Buenas noches, señorita Blanca, que calle es esta?"* Bloom asks him), whom he thinks might be a spy sent by the Citizen.

We're about to start spyralling into paranoia, A commented.

His suspicions give way to reproaches and feelings of guilt, the Cicerone said. His next visions are those of his parents, disguised as pantomime figures, his wife Molly dressed as an odalisque, Bridie Kelly the shilling whore he had his first sexual experience with, the lame Gerty MacDowell, now transformed into another cheap whore, and his friend and almost adolescent love Josie Breen.

Even allegories take shape in this phantasmagoric carnival, said C.

And the evocation of Molly and her love of the exotic gives place to tap-dancing singers who play the banjo, caper about, and then pull off their black minstrel masks and go cakewalking down the street, B said.

Followed by the dog, Bloom walks on to the junction of Mabbot and Tyrone Street, also known as the gates of hell, abandon all decency, the Cicerone said. Under an arch he sees a woman urinating standing up, leaning forward with her feet spread.

Leaning like a Tower of Pisa, A said. *U.p.: up.* so as not to lose sight of Mrs. Breen's husband.

Cheap whores at street entrances, corners, doorways, but Bloom continues on his way, the Cicerone said, trying to catch up with Stephen. On a wall he sees a phallic graffito and the words "Wet Dream." The dog turns into the ferocious Garryowen, and reluctantly Bloom gives him the pig's trotter and the lamb.

The dream or nightmare thickens, A said. The appearance of two watchmen leads Bloom to say first that he is his homonym, the dentist Bloom, but the card in his hatband gives him away as *Henry Flower*, said the Cicerone—of no fixed abode. His secret correspondent Martha Clifford is accusing him of breach of promise, and a trial begins that appears to have neither head nor tail, during which as in a relay race Bloom's fake identities pass the baton to each other, and the charges and prosecutors alternate, from Philip Beaufoy, author of the story Bloom read in the privy, to three punishing ladies who whip him, until he falls into the hands of the hangman and Master Barber Rumbold.

Blake said prisons were built with the stones of the law, Professor Jones said, and brothels with the bricks of religion. In this "Circe" brothel, law and religion both appear petrified in the figure of Sir Frederick Richard Falkiner (1831–1908), Recorder of Dublin, in his gray stone toga, who is also Michelangelo's *Moses*.

Bloom is saved from the unreal death sentence by a real English whore, A said. Zoe Higgins, no less. Zoe, which means "life" in Greek, and Higgins, Bloom's mother's maiden name.

Zoe Higgins, the girl from Yorkshire, in a sapphire slip, the Cicerone said, accosts Bloom when he halts in front of a lit-up house to listen to a piece of music that leads him to believe Stephen might be inside.

The whore hoarily handles his spud, said A. She takes it from him and also asks him for a fag. Bloom, who despite everything has retained his good sense, tells her there are better uses for a mouth. Go on, she tells him, "make a stump speech out of it" . . . that is, a campaign speech.

In a few moments, the Cicerone said, Bloom changes into a rabble-rouser who denounces the evils of the potato and tobacco, both brought by Sir Walter Raleigh from the New World. He then embarks on a meteoric political career: from mayor of Dublin to his coronation as emperor. Leopold I must reign over all the Irish without exception. Howard Parnell proclaims Bloom as the successor to his famous brother. Bloom is at the height of his power and builds the New Bloomusalem, the golden city. However, the mysterious man in the macintosh raises his voice to say Bloom is an impostor, the arsonist Leopold M'Intosh, whose real name is Higgins. After a sequence in which Bloom is the generous benefactor of the masses, another dissenting voice is heard. It is that of the preacher Alexander J. Dowie, the author of the pamphlet on the coming of Elijah, who now proclaims that Bloom is a hypocrite and worshipper of the Scarlet Woman. The crowd is enraged, and in spite of all Bloom's pleading and metamorphoses, turning into a woman to give birth to "eight male yellow and white children," he becomes the Messiah who has to be sacrificed.

A dead hand scribbles "Bloom is a cod" on the wall, said Professor Jones. A coded way of saying *God*? Bloom is a fish, the symbol of Christ. But *cod* can also be slang for "fool," or "nonsense," A said.

Bloom the scapegoat is stoned and burns in the Dublin firemen's bonfire, the Cicerone said. He is reborn from the flames like the phoenix, the new Messiah, while the daughters of Erin chant their litanies outlining the main themes of the novel.

Zoe finally helps Bloom get his feet back on the ground, A said, and attracts him with the "odour of her armpits" and the "lion reek" of her sex—or more precisely of the "male brutes that have possessed her." She manages to lure Bloom into the den of her madam Bella Cohen, where Stephen and Lynch are ensconced.

By now the color violet is dominant, B said, thanks to the light from the gas lamp in the music room, whose mantle is covered with mauve silk tissue paper.

Stretched out on a rug in front of the hearth, said the Cicerone, Lynch lifts the skirt and petticoat of Kitty Ricketts, "a bony pallid whore" who is perched on the edge of a table. Stephen is standing up, still hammering with two fingers on a pianola which the sleepy blonde in a tattered strawberry-colored gown listens to lolling on the sofa, her limp arm hanging down.

Florry Talbot, A said. A good name for a woman of the street. To help the conversation along, she says she has read in the press that the end of the world and the Antichrist are coming that summer. At that comes true pandemonium. Ragged newspaper sellers burst onto the scene, shouting the news of the arrival of the Antichrist. It is at this point that Stephen sees Bloom.

Among the many visions and mythical figures that appear and disappear, out of the chimney pops Bloom's grandfather, Lipoti Virag, "sausaged into several overcoats" and a macintosh. On his head is the double crown of Upper and Lower Egypt, the *pshent*—the new deity of writing and copying, as the two goose-quill feathers behind his ears testify. He has come to counsel his grandson in scientific and sexual matters. And above all in whores, A said—he's a real pornologist. The figure of Bloom's grandfather disguised as the outlandish Thoth could also be a cloak for Joyce himself and all his many layers, said Professor Jones.

More layers than an onion, A said. *L'ipotesi di lipoti* . . . the Lipoti hypothesis, he added. From Virag to virago. And then there's Bello—the dominant male Bella Cohen turns into in order to humiliate Bloom the masochist (who is probably called Leopold in honor of Sacher-Masoch).

Even the pinup girl from *Photo Bits* hanging in his bedroom turns up in the brothel to accuse Bloom of kissing her in four places, reporting too that he shaded her eyes, breasts, and private parts with pencil.

Let's draw a veil over that, said A. When Bloom thinks of Molly's "orangekeyed" chamber pot, we hear the sound of a cascading voice that says its name, *Poulaphouca*: the waterfall in the upper Liffey, some twenty miles southwest of Dublin.

Everything condemns Bloom, Professor Jones said. And to finish him off, Bella calls him a "Dead cod!," which is more than simply a dead fish: it implies something like impotence, because *cod*, in addition to the slang definitions mentioned earlier, can also mean "scrotum" or "testicle."

Death and resurrection, A said, because Bloom rallies, recovering his self-assurance and the potato-talisman Zoe Higgins took from him.

To increase the illicit associations in the brothel, Professor Jones said, Zoe's real name is Fanny, which was also Bloom's maternal grandmother's name. Her maiden name was Hegarty, and she married Julius Higgins.

Another more terrible grandmother will make her appearance at the end of "Circe," A said.

But where Bloom shows he has recovered his authority, responsibility, and astuteness, C said, is the moment when the prodigal son, Stephen, pays Bella Cohen a lavish thirty shillings for the three whores, and without realizing it gives her a pound too much. Bloom stops the robbery, pays Stephen's due in a lordly way, and makes sure he gets the change—one pound, six shillings, and eleven pence—so that Stephen does not lose it or pay any more than he owes.

Stephen attempts to light a cigarette, B said, but misses—after which he brings the flame close to his eye. "Lynx eye," says the shortsighted Stephen. He broke his glasses the day before and since then everything looks flat and blurred to him. Like an Impressionist, A said. In a paternal mood, Bloom advises him: "Don't smoke. You ought to eat." Stephen hasn't eaten a thing since that morning, and has drunk quite a bit, said C. That could be seen as a realistic explanation of the terrible hallucination he is about to suffer.

Before that terrible confrontation, A said, there is what I would call a communicating mirage in the brothel's hallway mirror. Stephen and Bloom look at each other in the mirror and see Shakespeare's beardless face in it, crowned by the antlers from the hat-stand. Note that the mirror reflects the antlers of the hat-stand, but not their own faces, said B. The faces of the real cuckold Bloom and the symbolic cuckold Stephen merge in the features of the great historical cuckold Shakespeare. The horns of the hat-stand and those of Bloom have already mingled shortly before this, when Blazes Boylan nonchalantly hangs his hat on Bloom's antlers. In this masochistic fantasy, Bloom is Boylan and Molly's lackey, A said, and they allow him to look through the keyhole at them making noisy love. Stephen makes fun of him in Latin, said Professor Jones, quoting the Vulgate: "*Et exaltabuntur cornua iusti.*"

Then the dance begins, A said, which becomes a *danse macabre*. Stephen waltzes with Zoe and then passes from Florry to Kitty, while Zoe grabs Florry, and then, releasing Kitty, Stephen begins a *pas seul*, dancing frenetically all on his own, perhaps doing a step similar to those Joyce used to break into when he was happy. They all waltz and wheel around entwined: Bloombella, Kittylynch, Florryzoe, and Stephen with his stick. Stephen and the room whirl round, the world turns on its axis, and suddenly Stephen stops: Ho!

Stephen's mother appears before him, B said. As a fearful leprous specter in a rotting bridal gown. She has no nose or teeth, and her eye sockets are empty . . .

She appears at night like the ghost in *Hamlet*, said Professor Jones.

Stephen asks his mother anxiously to tell him the word, C said: "The word known to all men." *Love*? Professor Jones asked. *Mother love*? *Mother*? That's the great recurring question in *Ulysses*. Perhaps the secret lies not so much in the word, said B, as in love itself. *Ulysses*, like Bloom, is love . . . said A in all seriousness.

But the only word that matters for Stephen's mother is prayer, B said. "I pray for you in my other world," she tells her son. She thinks solely of religious ritual . . .

Stephen's hallucination is perhaps the only one in the entire chapter that is realistic, C said. He has drunk a lot on an empty stomach. The others in the room only see that Stephen is dizzy and very white.

His mother's ghost goes on and on with her religious guff, but Stephen is bold enough to resist the farcical nonsense with three words: firstly, *Shite!*, then Lucifer's *Non serviam*, and finally

Nothung!, Siegfried's sword, which sounds almost like *Nothing*, as he raises his stick in both hands to strike the gas lamp.

Let there be darkness, B said. Stephen rushes out into the street, pursued by Lynch, Kitty, and Zoe.

Big Bella grabs Bloom by the coat-tails, the Cicerone went on. She demands ten shillings to pay for the lamp. Bloom is once more in control of the situation. He picks up Stephen's stick and points out that there isn't much damage, only the chimney of the lamp is broken. "There's not sixpenceworth of damage done." He cleverly insinuates to Bella that it is in her interest not to cause a fuss, because Stephen is a student at Trinity and knows important people. Trinity students are good clients of hers, after all—Bloom throws in a Masonic sign, just in case—and finally, to shut her up, he says he knows she has a son studying at Oxford. Bloom leaves in triumph, cloaked in a caliph's hood and poncho, and hurries down Tyrone Street in search of Stephen, "with fleet step of a pard," pursued by a phantasmagorical pack of bloodhounds.

At the corner of Beaver Street, Bloom stops to get his breath back, and hears Stephen and the two soldiers arguing nearby. These are the ones who poked fun at him at the start of the chapter; now one of them, Carr, accuses Stephen of molesting his girl, the shilling whore who is or claims to be Cissy Caffrey; the other, Compton, encourages his compatriot to smash Stephen's face in. Bloom pushes his way through the whores and tries to rescue Stephen, calling him professor. Then there is a series of misunderstandings about the home country and the king that ridicule jingoism and violence and conjure up several more fantastic apparitions, among others that of Edward VII, who passes himself off as the referee of the fight.

Instead of dying for his country, A said, Stephen shouts his slogan of peace: "Long live life!"

The mix-up over kings continues, said the Cicerone. New apparitions loom up, including the old milkmaid from the first chapter, now turned into a pantomime character, *Old Gummy Granny*, the representation of Ireland. She exhorts Stephen to resist to the death. Private Carr accuses Stephen of insulting his king; fresh apparitions file past; Lynch abandons Stephen, taking Kitty with him ("Exit Judas," Stephen says); Private Carr flings himself on Stephen and knocks him out with one blow.

This episode is based on an experience Joyce himself had, Professor Jones said. Shortly after he had met Nora, in St. Stephen's Green ("This is my green . . .") Joyce accosted a young girl, not noticing she was accompanied by a young man, who, as happens to Stephen in this chapter, knocked him down with one blow. And a supposed Jew who was passing by, called Alfred H. Hunter, who was being betrayed by his wife, played the Good Samaritan and came to the young Joyce's aid. For years the embryo of *Ulysses* was a short story Joyce never wrote that had Hunter as its main character.

Stephen lies flat on his back, said the Cicerone. His hat rolls away, and Bloom picks it up. Two watchmen arrive and Bloom, with the help of Corny Kelleher, the funeral director, succeeds in getting them to leave Stephen in peace.

Kelleher and Bloom try hypocritically to justify their presence in such a place, B said. Their lies are so far-fetched that Kelleher's carriage-horse neighs and laughs at them.

Carrying Stephen's hat and stick, Bloom shakes him by the shoulder, the Cicerone said. "Stephen!" he says, bringing his face close to the young man's. "Who?" asks Stephen, going on to mutter,

"Black panther. Vampire." These words, said Professor Jones, refer in turn to Haines's nightmare and the terrifying vision Stephen had of his mother, which he paraphrased by quoting a poem by Douglas Hyde back in "Proteus." He also quotes a few lines concerning one "Fergus," who Bloom thinks must be "Ferguson," the name of some girl or other, but in fact Stephen is reciting a lyric by W. B. Yeats, "Who Goes With Fergus," which Stephen sang for his mother on her deathbed.

Stephen's face reminds Bloom of the young man's poor mother, Mary Dedalus, said the Cicerone. While he is still standing protectively over him, the last apparition of "Circe" appears: a boy of eleven, dressed in an Eton suit, with glass slippers like Cinderella's and a helmet on his head. He is holding a book. "Rudy!" Bloom calls out silently.

The boy pushing up daisies has a crocus-colored face, said A, almost the same color as Stephen's.

After all the confusion, there is fusion, Professor Jones said. Bloom's dead son announces the birth of his new son. Bloom, the man-woman, finally gives birth to his longed-for son in the darkness of nighttown.

Do as Rudy does, A said. Keep quiet and go on reading.

Passageways

I

In a mirage of palm trees, the Cicerone said, an opulent Molly makes her apparition in Turkish costume and yashmak. So Stephen's premonitory dream comes true. Her ankles in chains, she offers herself submissively.

To stress the relationship with Stephen, she exclaims: "Nebrakada! Femininum!" Professor Jones explained—the spell Stephen read in a secondhand book in "Wandering Rocks." She also slaps the poor camel with a turban for turret that here represents Bloom. The tower is a phallic symbol, we're told, said A. A Martello to martyr oneself with. Omphalos or phallus?

II

At the start of Bloom's interior monologue in front of Zoe, the Cicerone said, there is a fantastic coronation procession: regiments, prelates, dignitaries from every church, representatives of every trade, from coopers and masseurs and funeral directors, to scriveners and chimneysweeps, all of them with their pennants and banners blowing in the wind . . .

It's an absolutely Rabelaisian list, C said.

And it includes lard refiners, said A. So that this carnival can have its Mardi Gras.

III

In another glorious impersonation, the Cicerone said, Bloom becomes the idol of women, who literally die for him. Some stab themselves, others hang themselves with their own garters, or fling themselves headfirst from Nelson's Pillar, or poison themselves . . .

And the Veiled Sibyl stabs herself, A said. She dies proclaiming, "My hero god!"

IV

In the obscene brothel scene, A said, the Cicerone is referring us back to what he said on page 210.

With his wand, Lynch lifts the navy skirt and white petticoat of the redheaded Kitty Ricketts, B said. She is wearing doeskin gloves and a chain purse, the height of elegance.

Lynch likes to poke the fire, A said. A little later he lifts his poker towards Zoe Higgins in her sapphire slip—she's the slippery sort—while she shows the dark clumps of hair in her armpits as she tries to light a cigarette in the gas lamp.

For the moment, Stephen does not use his ashplant, B said. It's with his hat on the pianola.

Zoe shows more than the hair under her arms, said C, because she isn't wearing any knickers.

V

Massive Bella Cohen begins her domination of Leopold the masochist, A said. She raises her skirt a little and offers Bloom the boot. He bends before her silk-encased leg and docilely ties the ribbon. One of Bloom's youthful dreams was to be an assistant in a shoe shop in Mansfield.

Bella, transformed into the mannish Bello, puts her heel on her servant Bloom's neck. "I promise never to disobey," says the submissive Bloom.

After beating and abusing Bloom, she squats on his face, strokes her hip, and blows smoke rings . . .

And uses poor Bloom's ear for an ashtray, B said.

VI

From the *Bath of the Nymph* hanging above the Gibraltar bed, A said, to this other bath in the hips of a whore, Bloom becomes quite immersed in his past as a Peeping Tom schoolboy, when he used his poor father's binoculars to spy on Lotty Clarke . . .

Obviously, A said, there's more here than meets the eye.

VII

The pianola is playing "My Girl's a Yorkshire Girl," said the Cicerone, and Bloom looks on as Stephen waltzes with the Yorkshire rose, Zoe Higgins, who sports a white vaccination scar on her upper arm. Round and round the room they spin. And through the curtains appears the foot of the dance teacher Denis Maginni, spinning his top hat on his toe. The foot is the mainstay of this chapter, said Professor Jones, because its organ is the locomotor apparatus. And dance, not just magic, is the art. And the top hat? asked A, provocatively. The top hat spins, said the Cicerone, and is a prelude to the "Waltz of the Hours" that Professor Maginni directs shortly afterward.

VIII

Stephen's frenetic "dance of death," the Cicerone said, comes to a sudden halt when his dead mother rises from the ground, her horrendous face barely covered by a torn bridal veil and a crown of withered orange blossoms, while Buck Mulligan, who insists to Stephen that his mother is "beastly dead," appears at the top of a tower dressed as a jester and holding a steaming bread-ball.

A scone, B corrected him, covered in butter. Perhaps it's for the sacrilegious communion of the living and the dead, said Professor Jones. *This is my scone . . .* A intoned.

IX

The milkmaid of the first chapter, the Cicerone said, reappears towards the end of this chapter disguised as *Old Gummy Granny*, the representation of poor, oppressed Ireland. She is sitting on a poisonous toadstool like the elves of Celtic folklore, "the death-flower of the potato blight on her breast." Stephen recognizes her immediately: "The old sow that eats her farrow!"

X

Pandemonium and final apocalypse in Stephen's agitated mind, said the Cicerone. There is chaos before he is knocked out, said A. Dublin burns, the Cicerone announced, birds of prey swoop from the sea and the bogs. Gangs of thieves rob the dying, the midnight sun darkens and the earth quakes, the dead in the Dublin cemeteries emerge from their graves in "white sheepskin overcoats and black goatfell cloaks." The hero Tom Rochford, who we are told in "Wandering Rocks" saved a workman from suffocating to death in a sewer, appears in vest and running shorts and runs off into the void pursued by a mass of runners. Elegant ladies (who've already booked their seats for the end of the world . . .) throw their skirts over their heads. Cackling witches in short skirts ("cutty sarks") ride through the air on broomsticks, the image imported from the poem "Tam o' Shanter" by Robert Burns (1759–1796). The chalice of a black mass stands on Mrs. Mina Purefoy's pregnant stomach. She has become the goddess of unreason. Father Malachi O'Flynn (who combines Mulligan with the Father O'Flynn of the famous ballad), with crossed feet and his chasuble inside out, celebrates the witches' sabbath, while the Reverend Hugh C. Haines Love (whose name now combines love and hate) holds an open umbrella over his head.

"Introibo ad altare diaboli," Father Malachi intones, thus closing the vicious circle opened that morning in the Martello tower.

PART THREE

16. EUMAEUS

Here are Bloom and Stephen, at the crucial point they found them-selves in at the end of the previous chapter, said the Cicerone, on the corner of Tyrone and Beaver Street. Bloom helps Stephen up, brushes the debris off him, hands him his hat and stick, and is now ready to start his return home, and the third part of the novel.

TITLE: Eumaeus	ORGAN: Nerves
SETTING: The cabman's shelter	TECHNIQUE: Narrative (old)
TIME: 12:40–1:15 A.M.	MEANING: The ambush at home
SCIENCE, ART: Navigation	CORRESPONDENCES:
	Eumaeus: "Skin-the-Goat" Fitzharris
SYMBOL: Sailors	Ulysses Pseudoangelos: the sailor Murphy
	Melanthius (Ulysses' disloyal goatherd): Corley
COLOR: Sepia	

Stephen expresses a desire for something to drink, said the Cicerone, and Bloom thinks he might be able to slake his thirst with milk and soda or mineral water at the cabman's shelter, not far from there on the quay by the Custom House, next to the railway bridge. They cannot find a cab, and so they walk along Amiens Street, turning by the back door of the morgue, and enter Store Street, famous for its police station at Number 3. With great satisfaction, Bloom breathes in the smell of our daily bread coming from James Rourke's bakery at numbers 5–6 Store Street, on the corner with Mabbot Street. As they are walking under the Loopline Bridge, Bloom tells Stephen someone has just saluted him: under the arches a tramp of medium height, wearing a battered hat and ragged clothes, has now raised his voice and greeted Stephen a second time. Bloom moves discreetly some distance away, but keeps a lookout. Even though he is not at his lucid best, Stephen recognizes the man as "Lord" John Corley, son of Inspector Corley, reduced to this lamentable state by his dissolute habits.

This Corley was the greedy beggar who was the companion of another wastrel, Lenehan, in the *Dubliners* story "Two Gallants," C said, although here he has fallen even lower.

The Cicerone said:

Corley tells Stephen the old story, that he is out of work, and Stephen says there will be a job the next day or the day after in Mr. Garret Deasy's school in Dalkey, but Corley says he is not cut out to be a teacher. "I have no place to sleep myself," Stephen tells him, and though he is famished, out of the kindness of his heart he feels in his pocket for a few pennies. As Corley points out, these turn out to be half-crowns, but Stephen lets him have one in any case. Corley then notices Bloom waiting nearby, and tells Stephen he has seen the man keeping company sometimes with Boylan in the Bleeding Horse, and asks if perhaps Bloom could recommend him for a job as a sandwich-board man with B.B. Stephen goes back to Bloom and tells him of Corley's request to be recommended to Boylan. Bloom stares at a dredger moored at the Custom House quay, and cautioning Stephen about Corley's type, advises the young man to return to his father's house, warning him further against Mulligan and other such bad company.

Near the cabman's shelter, they came across a group of men arguing loudly in Italian near an ice-cream cart. Beautiful language, Bloom says, once he and Stephen are inside the hut—"*Bella Poetria*," he effuses, meaning to say *bella poesia*—but Stephen replies dully that the men had merely been "haggling over money." Sounds are deceptive, he adds soon afterward.

Installed in the shelter, a wooden cafeteria of sorts run by the famous "Skin-the-Goat"* Fitzharris, who was said perhaps without reason to have been one of the Invincibles who took part in the Phoenix Park murders, Bloom asks for a cup of coffee and a bread roll because he thinks Stephen should eat something solid.

An old sailor with a red beard and a drinker's puffy eyes comes up to their table and introduces himself as D. B. Murphy, recently discharged from the *Rosevean*, the three-master Stephen contemplated from the beach in "Proteus." The sailor starts to tell a string of stories, each one more incredible than the last.

---

* So called because he apparently sold the skin of his pet goat to pay his drinking debts.

Murphy the sailor is a degraded parody of Ulysses himself, Professor Jones said. He says he has a faithful wife who has been waiting seven years for him in Carrigaloe, on a small island known as Great Island, near Cork. What's in a name, Stephen had asked shortly before this, quoting Shakespeare. One of the most common Irish surnames, "Murphy" can mean "potato," which is another link to Bloom-Ulysses. Murphy represents the *False-Messenger Ulysses, Odysseus Pseudoangelos*, from the title of a lost Greek comedy commented upon by Aristotle.

We cannot be sure in any case that the sailor is really called Murphy, the Cicerone said. Perhaps his name is as bogus as his adventures and journeys round the world. When he shows a postcard of Bolivian Indian women in loincloths, Bloom notices that it's addressed, with no message, to someone named A. Boudin . . .

Mr. Blood Pudding, C translated.

Amongst other bloodthirsty tales, the Cicerone said, Murphy or Boudin tells of how in a Trieste brothel he saw an Italian smuggler stick a knife up to the hilt in another smuggler's back—and as he tells the story, he pulls out another clasp knife just as big.

These traveler's tales make Bloom-Ulysses feel nostalgic, and he asks Murphy if he ever saw the Rock of Gibraltar.

The sailor's evasive reply—"I'm tired of all them rocks in the sea"—Professor Jones said, echoes Stephen's weary replies earlier, and the chapter's tired prose. It also brings us closer, *O, rocks!* to the beautiful lady from Gibraltar in Eccles Street.

After observing the amazing tattoo on Murphy's chest, Bloom sees with astonishment at the shelter door the face of the half-crazy streetwalker in the black straw hat he had avoided as he came out of the Ormond Hotel in "Sirens." He hides behind a copy of the *Evening Telegraph*, then launches into a series of observations to Stephen about the risks of venereal diseases due to the lack of medical checks on prostitutes. As well as providing scientific and moral advice, Bloom advises Stephen to drink his coffee and eat the bun that's as heavy as a brick. Stephen limits himself to sipping the coffee, and does not pay too much attention to Bloom's efforts to get him to eat.

After commenting on the stabbing in the Trieste brothel, Bloom begins a series of commonplaces about the passionate temperament of southern peoples, especially Spaniards, who are prone to taking justice into their own hands. "Climate accounts for character," says Bloom, and tells Stephen his own wife is half Spanish, as she was born in what was technically Spain, that is, Gibraltar. And she is the Spanish type: dark-skinned, black-haired . . . Molly's generous curves lead him to the sculpted Mediterranean beauties he contemplated a few hours earlier in the Kildare Street museum. They are different from the Irish woman of today, who, he says, do not dress well, in general; and Bloom points out he particularly dislikes seeing a woman with rumpled stockings.

The general conversation dies away at this point, being concentrated mostly on naval voyages and shipwrecks, until thanks to Bloom it turns toward the subject of Jews (Spain began to fall into decline when it expelled them, Bloom noted) and Ireland, a nationalist theme of no interest to the bored Stephen, who concludes: "We can't change the country. Let us change the subject." At this, Bloom starts to peruse the copy of the *Telegraph*, and when he reads the report of Dignam's funeral, drawn up by Hynes, he discovers that, thanks to an erratum, he has been listed as *L. Boom*. He also sees that Stephen Dedalus is mentioned as having been present at the funeral. This error doesn't seem to interest Stephen much either, and he yawns again. While he reads the letter from Mr. Deasy about foot-and-mouth disease on page two, Bloom reads on page three about the Ascot Gold Cup, won by Throwaway.

The talk in the shelter then turns to the inevitable Parnell and his legend. Bloom remembers the great moment in his life when he picked up Parnell's silk hat and was rewarded with an unforgettable "Thank you." Mention is also made of Kitty O'Shea, the woman who was Parnell's ruin. Bloom mistakenly says she was Spanish, which gives him the opportunity to return to the question of the Spanish character. He shows Stephen a somewhat soiled photo of Molly, of the *prima donna* Madam Marion Tweedy, standing in a low-cut evening gown next to a piano on whose stand lies the music for "In Old Madrid," a ballad that was in fashion in those days, around 1896. Looking at the opulent curves in the photo, he is reminded of other soilings, the soiled linen that is even more enchanting than the freshly starched, in her untidy bedroom. The terrible thought strikes him, "Suppose she was gone when he?," but he dismisses it, remembering an image from that same morning reminding him of their conjugal routine and stability: on the bedroom floor, the novel *Ruby: The Pride of the Ring* (which had prompted Molly's question about the *met him pike hoses* or metempsychosis), which had fallen down beside the chamber pot.

Astounded to discover that Stephen has not eaten for more than twenty-four hours—his last proper meal was dinner on Wednesday, and now it is almost one o'clock on Friday morning—Bloom plucks up his courage (because he recalls the problems that arose when he brought a stray dog with a wounded paw home one night) and invites the apathetic and appetite-less young man back to Eccles Street with him. It is nearby, and there they can have a cup of cocoa and go on talking in a more relaxed atmosphere.

Just as he did with the dog with a wounded paw, Professor Jones said, he is now going to take Stephen home. Stephen does in fact have a damaged hand, perhaps the result of a fight with Mulligan when they separated at Amiens Street station at the end of "Oxen of the Sun." To underscore the symmetries, we should not forget that Mulligan called Stephen "dogsbody."

Bloom pays fourpence for the coffee and roll, the Cicerone said, and goes out with his young companion. The night air and the walk will do Stephen good, Bloom tells the latter, and takes his arm to help him on his way.

As they cross Beresford Place, they begin talking about music. Bloom likes light, melodic pieces, without Wagnerian complexities. His favorite composers are Mercadante, Meyer, and Mozart, although he does especially admire Rossini's *Stabat Mater*, a work in which Madam Marion Tweedy shone splendidly in a performance at the Jesuit Church in Upper Gardiner Street. Stephen's tastes are more rarefied. He praises Shakespeare's songs, the English lutenist John Dowland (1563–1626), and said that he himself was thinking of buying a lute from Mr. Arnold Dolmetsch of London—as Joyce himself tried to do in 1904. He also applauds the seventeenth-century English songwriter Giles Farnaby (and his son Richard) and the organists of the same period and country: William Byrd, Thomas Tomkins, and John Bull.

They pass by a poor horse pulling a sweeper that is making a lot of noise, and Bloom wonders if this John Bull was the same man as the same-named political celebrity. Looking at the horse's weary head, Bloom is sorry not to have a lump of sugar to give it. Shortly afterward, he asserts that his wife, who is so passionately fond of all kinds of music, would be delighted to make the acquaintance of a young man so well-versed musically—and as gifted vocally as his father Simon Dedalus, Bloom discovers at once, when Stephen bursts into the first two lines of a song by the German choirmaster and composer Johannes Jeep (c. 1582–1650) about the sea and sirens.

Stephen's beautiful tenor voice immediately wins Bloom over, and he starts hatching fantastic plans for Stephen's musical education. He sees a brilliant musical career ahead of Stephen if he allows himself to be properly guided and stays away from bad company like Mulligan—and besides, this lucrative profession would leave the young man lots of free time to pursue literature, which would itself prove no hindrance whatever to his vocal career.

At this point, the horse stops, lifts its tail, and lets drop one, two, three steaming turds.

Three ones make three, Professor Jones said. To complete the trinity, let us not forget that this Third Part of *Ulysses* begins, "Preparatory to anything else," with the *P* of "Poldy," as Molly affectionately calls her husband.

Passageways

I

On the dangerous corner of Tyrone and Beaver Street, the Cicerone pointed out with his wand, while still in nighttown, Bloom
hands hat and stick to Stephen, through whose still unsteady
mind the vampire of a poem scrawled the previous morning on
the beach at Sandymount has just fluttered.

II

Under the Loopline Bridge, near the Custom House quay, said
the Cicerone, Stephen halts in front of a pile of cobblestones and,
by the light of a coke brazier, is able to make out the dark shadow

of a municipal watchman in his sentry box. Despite his fuzzy mind, it does not take him long to recognize the watchman as Gumley, a former friend of his father's, and one of the Invincibles who in 1882 took part in what were known as the Phoenix Park Murders, when the Secretary of State for Ireland, Lord Frederick Cavendish, and the Deputy Secretary Thomas Henry Burke, were assassinated.

To avoid meeting Gumley, Stephen walks nearer the pillars of the railway bridge.

In real life, the watchman was another Invincible, James Fitzharris, who was not in fact the owner of the cabman's shelter.

III

Inside the cabman's shelter, the Cicerone said, the bearded drunken sailor Murhpy, with huge bags under his eyes, stares quizzically at Bloom and Stephen—who cannot bring himself to try the prehistoric bread and the dishwater served as coffee, even though Bloom keeps surreptitiously pushing the cup under his nose.

IV

Unbuttoning his shirt, Seaman Murphy shows the customers in the cabman's shelter the tattoo on his chest, which represents the number sixteen and the outline of a young man's frowning face, said the Cicerone, tracing the shape with his wand.

Murphy explains in great detail that the tattoo was done for him by a Greek called Antonio, whose self-portrait it was, when their ship was lying becalmed off Odessa. Murphy enjoins the crowd to watch Antonio as he makes the face smile, pulling the skin taut. Unfortunately, "He's gone too," says Murphy: "Ate by sharks after."

The number sixteen probably represents an erotic figure in Greek love—Greek like Antonio, said Professor Jones. And of course it has many numerological connotations.

It's enough to recall that we are in chapter 16, C said, and that Bloomsday is June 16, and that Bloom is sixteen years older than Stephen.

V

In the end, persuaded by Bloom to at least try it, Stephen raises the heavy cup from its brown pool and takes a sip of the dishwater.

VI

Bloom proudly shows Stephen the photo of Molly in her evening gown next to the piano, the Cicerone said. He explains that the photograph does not do justice to her figure in that *toilette*, and that a full-length portrait would have been better, so as not to over-emphasize certain opulent curves . . . Bloom is on the point of going out for a few moments on the pretext of needing to urinate—in order to let the young man feast his eyes on the sight—but eventually he simply turns his head away, thoughtfully, so as not to inhibit the appreciation of such beauty.

VII

As they leave the cabman's shelter, Bloom asks Stephen to lean on him, the Cicerone said, and so Ulysses and Telemachus return home arm-in-arm.

And so tic-tac-toe to Ithaca, exclaimed A, who had remained silent, agreeing or nodding off throughout the entire chapter, between beautiful B and the enigmatic man with the Macintosh, who were both as silent as he.

17. ITHACA

Who asks the 309 questions, and who gives the 308 replies and one silence that make up chapter 17 of *Ulysses*?

The book itself, an encyclopedia that bites its own tale but not its tongue (even managing to parody itself) and catechize (instruct) its readers by going over ancient events, revealing new ones, and correcting some few mistakes.

For example?

There is a recapitulation of Bloom's odyssey, from "Calypso" to the present chapter, as if it were a Jewish ritual. It is revealed that Bloom and Stephen were baptized in the same church, that of the Three Patrons, in Rathgar Road, and by the same vicar, the Reverend Charles Malone. The correct address for Bella Cohen's brothel is given, at 82 Tyrone Street, Lower, whereas in "Circe" it had figured as number 81.

Is the system of questions and answers in this chapter based on the catechism?

The catechism of an Aesthete Father, occasionally encyclopedantic, who like Stephen Dedalus was very familiar with the textbook *Historical and Miscellaneous Questions for the Use of Young People, with a Selection of British and General Biography*, by Richmal Mangnall, and was obsessed by the correctness of the facts he was employing, as is shown by the letters to his Aunt Josephine verifying details about Dublin—such as, for example, whether it would be possible for Bloom to get into his house by climbing down the entrance railing to the semi-basement kitchen at the start of this chapter, which was Joyce's favorite and which he called the "ugly duckling," perhaps because of its odd appearance.

ULYSSES III.17.doc

TITLE: Ithaca

SETTING: The Bloom family home (7 Eccles Street)

TIME: 1:15–2:50 A.M.

SCIENCE, ART: Science

SYMBOL: Comets

COLOR: Starry milky

ORGAN: Skeleton

TECHNIQUE: Catechism (impersonal)

MEANING: Armed hope

CORRESPONDENCES:
Ulysses: Bloom
Telemachus: Stephen
Eurimacus the Suitor: Boylan
Antinous the Suitor: Mulligan
Suitors: Scruples
Bow: Reason

Suddenly the best of friends, Bloom and Stephen walk over to Eccles Street from Beresford Place. The Cicerone pointed out their route on a map of Dublin. They go in a straight line along

Gardiner Street, Lower and Middle, skirt Mountjoy Square, then turn left into Gardiner Place, and then right along Temple Street North, crossing Hardwicke Place and finally reaching 7 Eccles Street in the northwest of the city.

During their walk they talk of music, literature, Ireland, Dublin, Paris, friendship, women, and prostitution, among other things, and Stephen's collapse as well—something the two cannot agree about, because Bloom the scientist puts it down to a lack of sustenance made worse by an excess of alcohol, whereas the artist-theologian Stephen blames the reappearance of a cloud both of them had observed at the same time that morning from different viewpoints (a practical illustration of the parallax that had intrigued Bloom at various moments during the day), at first seeming no bigger than a woman's hand—a detail that perhaps, in Professor Jones's view, refers to the cloud the size of a man's hand that brings the rain prayed for by the prophet Elijah in 1 Kings 18:44, and is also a reminder of Stephen's dead mother, whom he thought of as he gazed at the cloud from the Martello tower that morning.

Among the qualities linking Stephen and Bloom discovered by the latter, such as a greater sensitivity towards music than the plastic arts, preferring life on a continent to that on an island, skepticism toward religious and political orthodoxies, and attraction toward the opposite sex, might also be included the lack of a key, the fact of being "keyless," if it can be so termed, as Bloom discovers to his annoyance when he reaches his house. This however proves no hindrance to his resourceful mind, because using a strategy worthy of Ulysses, he finally succeeds in gaining access to his conjugal home without waking his wife, climbing over a railing and letting his whole body-weight of a hundred and fifty-eight pounds drop into the tiny yard in front of the semi-basement. He goes into the kitchen, lights the gas lamp and, candle in hand, goes upstairs to let Stephen in through the front door. Guiding him along the hallway and leaving behind on the left the strip of light under the door of the bedroom where Molly lies sleeping, the two men go down five steps and enter the kitchen.

Bloom blows out the candle, sets out two chairs for Stephen and himself, turns on the tap at the sink, and half fills a black iron kettle with water that has come to his home from the Roundwood reservoir, which he puts on the coal fire of the hob. He then returns to the sink to wash his hands with "a partially consumed tablet of Barrington's lemonflavoured soap," which has accompanied him on his odyssey from Sweny's, ablutions which Stephen declines because of his congenital lack of hygiene, according to B, a hydrophobia which Professor Jones saw as a characteristic of saints and geniuses, and which in Stephen's case is also the symbol of his rejection of being baptized. Which did not however prevent Professor Jones from declaring that the true communion in the novel, following the failed attempts to celebrate Mass by the bogus priest Mulligan in the Martello tower and Bella Cohen's brothel, takes place in this chapter when Bloom prepares two cups of Epps's cocoa. To underline hospitality, equality, and fraternity, Bloom declines to use the moustache cup his daughter Milly had given him, and instead chooses an identical cup to the one his guest is using. He also pours into Stephen's cup more of the cream reserved for Molly's breakfast. Drinking the cocoa gives rise to a string of calculations, reflections, and revelations, among which are the fact that Bloom and Stephen had previously met on two occasions: the first in 1887, when Stephen was five years old and was with his mother in the garden of Matthew Dillon's house, and he refused to shake Bloom's hand; the second five years later, one rainy Sunday in the cafe of Breslin's hotel at the seaside resort of Bray, when Stephen was with his father and his great-uncle. It occurred to the boy to invite Bloom to dine with them, an invitation seconded by his father but declined with exquisite tact and politeness by Bloom.

After going over some similarities and coincidences between Bloom and Stephen, the idea of communion is reinforced with the discovery of the composite names *Stoom* and *Blephen*.

At the same time, the differences between their two temperaments are not overlooked: one is scientific, the other artistic; plus Bloom is Jewish and Stephen a gentile, as the cruel ballad that Stephen sings demonstrates. It tells of how the little boy Harry Hughes was playing ball and broke a windowpane in the house of a Jew, so the man's daughter, dressed all in green, asked the boy in and then cut off his head with a penknife. The song brings the image of his daughter Milly, dressed in green, to Bloom's mind, as well as several memories of her childhood and the object lessons he gave her, using wedding gifts such as a stuffed owl and a clock.

Perhaps moved by these filial evocations, but above all to start destroying the "suitor" Boylan with Telemachus-Stephen's help, Bloom invites the young man to spend the night in the house. (A said parenthetically that Bloom is being rather cynical when, after considering him for his daughter, he asks if Stephen knows a Mrs.

Sinico, because in the *Dubliners* story "A Painful Case," Captain Sinico puts a Mr. Duffy up in his house because he thinks the latter is interested in his daughter, when in reality it is the mother he has eyes for . . .).

Stephen promptly refuses this invitation, but expresses his gratitude and friendship. Bloom returns the one pound and seven shillings he had recovered from the brothel for Stephen, and the two men agree Stephen should give Molly Italian lessons. In return, she would give Stephen singing lessons, while the two of them, Bloom and Stephen, will meet frequently to discuss intellectual topics of mutual interest. However, deep down both of them know these plans are an illusion, and would be hard to put into practice.

In fact, Bloom knows that finding a new "son" is also likely to prove a very fleeting illusion, C said, but what is stronger and longer lasting is the sense of brotherhood that he has probably succeeded in arousing in the proud, egocentric Stephen.

Stephen put on his hat, and the pair of them went out into the garden to contemplate "the heaventree of stars hung with humid nightblue fruit."

A riveder le stelle, the pedant Professor Jones exclaimed, going on to point out that when Bloom and Stephen are about to go out into the garden, Stephen sings the psalm "In exitu Israel de Egipto," as sung by the souls that Dante and Virgil see arriving in *Purgatory*.

But Bloom and Stephen have also gone outside to urinate, A said, and to look up at the light in Molly's window.

Bloom opens the garden gate, the two men shake hands (the gesture that should have happened seventeen years earlier, B observed) the bells of the nearby church of Saint George strike two (reminding Stephen of his dead mother, and Bloom of Dignam's funeral and several other companions), at which Stephen, ineluctable modality of the invisible, disappears into the night.

Left alone, Bloom feels the cold of interstellar space that so terrified Pascal, the weight and sorrow of his own solitude or "lonechill," and wonders whether he ought to remain outside on the lookout for the gradual disappearance of the stars and the arrival of dawn and sunrise. Breathing in deeply, he returns inside, and in the front room bangs his head against a sideboard, because Molly has moved various pieces of furniture around. Something else besides the furniture has changed in the house, and so Bloom lights a tiny incense cone to perfume the atmosphere (reinforcing the analogy with Ulysses, Professor Jones said, because he too fumigated his house after massacring all the suitors), then looks at himself in the gilt-framed mirror over the hearth, which also reflects the books in his library, some of which have been turned upside down by Molly, and which Bloom now turns back the right way up.

While Bloom is undressing, we see the accounts (debit/credit) for his day. We can see his incomes, for example the commission received from the *Freeman* (one pound seven and six), and his outgoings, in which the cost of transport to nighttown and the eleven shillings spent in Bella Cohen's brothel are not recorded.

After that, Bloom places his flat right foot on the edge of a chair seat, picks off a protruding part of his big toenail, and smells it happily because the smell takes him back to his infancy and arouses his fantasies of an ideal home. This reverie seems inspired less by the magazine *Ideal Home* than to have come straight out of the pages of *Bouvard and Pécuchet*, C observed. Then Bloom fantasizes further about different hobbies and pursuits he is interested in, such as photography, astronomy, the comparative study of religions, eroticism, the produce and livestock appropriate to the life of a gentleman farmer, inventions, industrial activities—a host of schemes that would be difficult to put into practice and in the end are reduced to the practical ambition of succeeding in creating an ad that would bring passersby to a halt in wonder. Let's hope he finds the key or keys to his ad some day, said B.

For now though, the Cicerone went on, Bloom unlocks a very private drawer where he keeps a variety of souvenirs, such as Milly's handwriting book, an old hourglass, newspaper cuttings, leaflets, pornographic photos, stamps, and three typewritten letters with the name and address of the sender written in the following cryptogram:

N. IGS. / WI. UU. OX / W. OKS. MH / Y. IM

What is this alphabet soup? asked B with a frown. Almost at once, the answer flashed on the screen:

M.RTH. / DR.FF.LC / D.LPH.NS / B.RN

The flight of the vowels, C said, then watched as they were filled in:

MARTHA / DROFFILC / DOLPHINS / BARN

The surname Clifford has been inverted for greater security, Professor Jones said, in this cryptogram of an inverted alphabet.

But we still do not know who Martha Clifford really is, B said, unless her real name is the one she gave in her appearance in "Circe": Peggy Griffin.

Yes, Griffin, A said. Perhaps she's the sister of the Invisible Man . . .

The real invisible man in his cloak will soon make a reappearance, C said.

Bloom adds Martha Clifford's fourth letter to his collection, said the Cicerone, reflecting that he can still create a favorable impression in persons of the opposite sex, as Mrs. Breen, Nurse Callan, and Gerty MacDowell had shown during the course of his odyssey.

Bloom opens a second drawer. It contains various documents: a birth certificate for Leopold Paula Bloom [*sic*], insurance policies, a press cutting announcing the change of name of Rudolph Virag, henceforth to be known as Bloom, a daguerreotype of Rudolph Virag and his father Leopold Virag, his father's farewell letter when he committed suicide—because he could not bear the loneliness after his wife's death. Thinking of the words in the letter brings on a mood of sadness and melancholy, in which Bloom sees himself in the grip of poverty. He even tells himself it would be better for him to leave his house and failed marriage, and goes on to list the possible places he could go, including Gibraltar, where his wife was born. Then thanks to memories of her, he sees the Plaza de Toros at La Línea de la Concepción. He could become a real Wandering Jew-Ulysses (*The Wandering Ulysses*, A said), he would wander forever, become an Everyman and Noman until he disappears into interstellar space like a mythological character. But tiredness leads him to put his feet back on the ground and head for bed.

Among the frustrations of the day, the question he has not been able to find an answer to returns to haunt him: "Who was M'Intosh?"

When he goes into the bedroom, Bloom sees several articles of Molly's clothing (a pair of black stockings, a pair of violet garters, a pair of knickers smelling of opoponax, jasmine, and Muratti's Turkish cigarettes, a blue moiré silk petticoat . . .) thrown on top of a trunk that had once belonged to Brian Cooper Tweedy, Molly's father, as indicated by the initials on the front.

Bloom finishes undressing, puts on his nightshirt, and cautiously gets into bed. He realizes that there is the imprint of a male body that is not his on the mattress, and that on the fresh, clean sheets there are some crumbs and bits of potted meat. This leads him to reflect on fidelity, jealousy, and envy, and he draws up a mental list of all Molly's lovers, twenty-five in all, from the first, Mulvey, to Boylan, including the mayor of Dublin, Simon Dedalus, Professor Goodwin, and Father Bernard Corrigan . . .

It seems likely that the only real lover Molly had, in the full sense of the word, was Boylan, C said.

Bloom's list is in some way an homage, Professor Jones said, a list of worshippers of the Great Mother.

It seems to me, B said, that this list of Molly's lovers, most of them highly improbable and some of them technically impossible, is possibly an unconscious attempt by Bloom to deny truth and reality to the only real lover—or at least the only one that matters to him—Boylan. By mixing him up with the unreal ones, he becomes less real too.

What is most important, A said, is that Bloom, at the end of his odyssey, ends up resigning himself to the human condition. He accepts the world as it is, with its two hemispheres, east and west, as they are memorably represented in the two melons of Molly's buttocks, on which he plants a kiss, his great Yes to life.

Bloom does the same as Ulysses, who kissed the ground when he found he was in Ithaca once more.

Bloom's kiss wakens Molly. In her sleepy state, the Cicerone said, she asks him what he did during the day, and Bloom goes over it, leaving out a few more or less dubious events, such as his secret correspondence with Martha Clifford, the fight at Kiernan's pub, his masturbation on the beach . . . and stressing above all his meeting with Stephen Dedalus, "professor and author." Molly makes a mental list of her husband's deficiencies, including his "abandonment" of her: She remembers the exact date of the last time he fulfilled his conjugal duty: November 27, 1893. Bloom, for his part, reflects that spiritual and intellectual relations between them had recently been lacking. Possibly both of them need to make an effort, and perhaps for this reason he asks Molly, as we learn at the start of the next chapter, to do something she has not done since the good old days—to bring him breakfast in bed in the morning.

Now as man and wife lie in bed, him with his feet at the top, next to her head—a position Joyce liked to adopt at a certain point in his life—the voyage of *Ulysses* comes to a close.

The traveler, a bent Sinbad, said a ventriloquist's voice, adopts a fetal position in the roc's egg and the cosmic egg of night (a couple of scrambled eggs, sir), the two poles (Yin and Yang) flatten in the squaring of the circle (he's already kissed the ass of the world) and in the circling of the square of the bed of the Great Geometrician (*Gea Mater*). The earth turns and turns around the final question[*] (axle), which is answered in analogical mode (eye) with a great full stop that is a fresh start (though this remains to be seen), returning to the point of everlasting return:

Where?

---

[*] Where's the man with the Macintosh? B exclaimed, staring at the computer screen, switched on but abandoned at the door to Room 18.

Passageways

I

Did he fall?

Bloom falls, with the leaden weight of his humanity, when he jumps down into the yard in front of the semi-basement. But more permanent is the symbolic fall . . .

II

What does Stephen see through the kitchen windows?

A man regulating a gas flame who, four minutes later, reappeared with a candle to show him in through the front door of 7 Eccles Street.

III

What high quality products are there on the middle shelf of the kitchen dresser that Bloom opens?

An empty pot of Plumtree's Potted Meat (which Molly and Boylan ate in bed, having just "potted some meat" of their own), a packet of soluble Epps's cocoa (*Theobroma cacao*, or food of the gods with which Bloom and Stephen celebrate communion—a variety deliberately referred to as a "massproduct": a product for the masses but also for a Mass), a jar of Irish Model Dairy's cream, which Molly is no doubt going to miss the following morning, if she isn't too busy making breakfast for her Poldy.

What attracts Bloom's attention on the ledge of the dresser?

Four fragments of two tickets. In the next chapter we will learn who tore them up and why.

IV

What visual recollections does Bloom have of his adolescence?

He spent the empty hours looking through "a rondel of bossed glass of a multicoloured pane" at the ever-changing spectacle of the street: "pedestrians, quadrupeds, velocipedes," different kinds of vehicles . . .

V

How do Stephen and Bloom establish a comparison between the Irish and Hebrew languages?

By juxtaposition. On the penultimate blank page of the novel *The Sweets of Sin*, Stephen writes in pencil the simple and modified Irish characters corresponding to the letters *G, E, D,* and *M*, and Bloom then in turn wrote the Hebrew characters "ghimel, aleph, daleth and (in the absence of mem) a substituted qoph . . ."

The union in the here and now becomes hieroghamic on *The Sweets of Sin*, Professor Jones said, though the oghamic script is here substituted for by the simple and modified Irish characters . . .

VI

What shared activity do Bloom and Stephen engage in immediately after they both notice the light of a paraffin lamp in the window of Molly's bedroom?

They urinate.

How?

Standing up, of course. *U.p.: up.* Elbow to elbow, their "organs of micturition" invisible to each other thanks to "manual circumposition."

What considerations fill the minds of each of them, encouraged by the other's invisible audible organ?

In Bloom's case, anatomical and physiological considerations about his virile member, in Stephen's case, considerations about Jesus's circumcision and the divine foreskin.

Stephen is wrong to think that because Bloom is a Jew he had been circumcised, said B.

The act of urinating together, C said, is both a competition outside Molly's window and a demonstration of mutual confidence and friendship.

Before the conclusion of this penultimate chapter, B said, the trajectory of Bloom's urine almost has the shape of the penultimate letter of the alphabet.

The Greek *Y* to sign the odyssey of the Greekjew, A said.

In Joyce, urine is often associated with the act of writing and is considered creative, Professor Jones said. See for example how indelible ink is made in *Finnegans Wake*.

The Sweets of Orion, C said. *Pssst!*

Miction accomplished, A said.

VII

What did Bloom contemplate on the upright piano made in England by Charles Cadby's piano factory?

A long yellow pair of Molly's gloves; "an emerald ashtray containing four consumed matches," one Muratti cigarette, partially consumed, and two discolored butts. On the music stand the score of "Love's Old Sweet Song" opened at the last page with the final indications *ad libitum, forte, animato, ritirando* . . .

I would concentrate on the *ad libitum*, Professor Jones said. As the pianist wishes.

I would concentrate on the ashtray, B said.

Polluted by Boylan, A said. Let's move on to the *ritirando* . . .

Love is the sweetest of all songs. That's how "Love's Old Sweet Song" ends, B said, humming. "Love will be found the sweetest song of all."

The sweets of the sin of loving, said A.

18. PENELOPE

Yes, B agreed with what A had just so roundly affirmed: it's those breasts, because from the start we are deliberately shown the round-ness of Molly's robust bust—and Professor Jones went on making extravagant curvilinear gestures with his great paws outside the door to the last room in the house-museum of *Ulysses*, as if he too

```
●○○                          ULYSSES III.18.doc

TITLE: Penelope                    ORGAN: Flesh

SETTING: The bed                   TECHNIQUE: Monologue (female)

TIME: 2:50–3:33 A.M.               MEANING: The past sleeps

SCIENCE, ART: ——                   CORRESPONDENCES:
                                   Penelope: Molly
SYMBOL: Earth                      Ulysses: Bloom

COLOR: Milky—then new dawn
```

had lost his tongue, although in the end he got abreast of the situation and according to Joyce, the first cardinal point in this chapter—cardinal point and food fit for a cardinal, A said—at least for Boylan, who that afternoon took a good bite at Molly's fat savorsome breasts, which, B reminded us, during the feeding of Milly also sweetened Bloom's life and lips, himself proud of this lacteal delectation, A went on, and who even wanted to milk them into his teacup, he added, ready to embark on a horrid comparison that Professor Jones cut off with a cutting No!, and the reverberations echoed like the thunderclap that woke and frightened Molly at ten the previous night in her adulterous bed, the same thunder that scared Stephen in the hospital in the "Oxen of the Sun" chapter, both of them as terrified of storms as they are of their creator, "God be merciful to us," Molly thought the sky was falling in on her for everything she had done that afternoon with Boylan, sexual congress fortified with potted meat and port, A said, and when Molly crossed herself she was reminded of the tremendous thunderstorms in Gibraltar ("as if the world was coming to an end" there where the world ends), what better proof of the existence of God for a believer like Molly, C said, a sound not all that different from the shout in the street that is God for Stephen, B observed, and from the candle she lit one night in the Carmelite Chapel on Whitefriars Street she passes almost without transition, A pointed out, to Boylan's thick candle, his stallion prick, C corrected him, she had never seen anything so big, A emphasized, although in fact, B said, before then she had probably only made love to Bloom and Boylan, but in all likelihood she has seen and handled the candles of other men, A said, although not as many as those Bloom put on his list, perhaps only that of her first love, B said, the Lieutenant Mulvey in the navy who she jerked off on the rock of Gibraltar, and that of a Lieutenant Gardner, A said, also in Gibraltar, and probably that of the tenor Bartell d'Arcy, said C, and also possibly that of—but with a wave of his wand the Cicerone cut short the list, inviting us to step inside the milky-way room of the lady of the night, curious isn't it, B went on, what a maneater Molly is usually seen as, even though her sex life has been quite limited, but not her appetite, A said, and in fact the image we have of Molly at the start of the chapter is the one formed or deformed by Bloom and a few comments made by male gossips, the first and almost only thing we've heard directly from her, B said, is a grunt "Mn" and then the orders she gave Poldy, for many readers and critics, even some feminists, C observed, Molly is some sort of virago, and they prefer her husband, the female man, a racist and *machista* concept, Professor Jones observed, applied by the philosopher Otto Weininger in his book *Sex and Character* (1903) to the Jews, yes there are almost as many Mollys as there are readers, B said, some see her as contradictory, C said, that's how she is, B said, the Great Mother and the Great Whore, said C, that was more or less how Joyce saw his Nora, the main model for Molly, Professor Jones said, in a letter he told her that at certain moments he saw her as the Virgin or Madonna but then immediately saw her as "shameless, insolent, half naked and obscene," that's my Molly, A said, but instead of Nora's image we should look at her writing, Joyce knew that style makes the woman and for Molly's monologue he was inspired by Nora's letters, particularly in their almost complete lack of punctuation and certain spelling mistakes, C said, her careless naturalness, A said, more natural than nature itself, Professor Jones said, an anti-Freudian professor called her hysterical, C said, others would say she is polymorphously perverse, *merverse Mollymorphe!* A exclaimed in something like French, but her sexual experiences are pretty normal, B said, an ambiguous flirtation in adolescence with a young female friend in Gibraltar, masturbations, *coitus oralis, interruptus, in anum*, Professor Jones detailed, almost no reader sees her as a housewife, said B, few see her as a mother, and few remember that on this *Ulysses* day she remembers Rudy's death, ten years, five months, and seven days earlier, C recalled, a day that changed Molly and Bloom's lives profoundly, they both still want a son, A said, they could stand to look after Milly a little more, B suggested, on the 15th she turned 15, Molly's relationship with her daughter is as contradictory as that with her husband, C said, some people see Molly as an archetype, but the truth is she's as complex as most women, A said, and most men, said B, Molly is a mystery, A said, the fact is we know little about her past, B said, almost nothing about her mother the Spanish Jew Lunita Laredo who probably abandoned her and her father, Professor Jones ventured, her father Commander Tweedy was possibly only a sergeant, B said, even the Gibraltar bed that the contradictory Molly both likes and dislikes in fact had a much less illustrious origin, C said—in the bed that belonged to a Cohen there is now a Bella, A said—she's Bloom's dominatrix, C said, but she also likes to be dominated, B said, to tame and be tamed, said A, beloved dove and woman of the street, Professor Jones said, sensitive and vulgar at one and the same time, who calls a spade a spade and the penis a prick, A said, but contrary to what is generally believed, said C, there are not that many "dirty" words in *Ulysses*, for example *fucked* appears only twice in the entire novel, "fucked yes and damn well fucked too," B recited, as Molly has it, it would be easy to destroy Molly's good name by concentrating on her negative aspects, B went on, to demolish her, said A, but she is also the rose of Castile who wants the whole house to be flooded with roses, B said, and she has a charitable soul in a generous body, A said, we saw her arm emerge from the window to throw some money to the lame sailor, said C, and we also see her pretty foot awakening the desires of both Boylan and Poldy, A said, or we see her like a new Penelope knitting the shroud for her little son Rudy, C said, Molly is many Mollys, said B, every reader sees something of him or herself in *their* Molly, C said, to some she is the average sensual woman—or more than average, A added—to others she is stupid, ignorant and amoral, C went on, but she isn't stupid in any way sense or form, declared B, its true she isn't very educated, and confuses Alias with Ananias, B said, winking at A, or gets in a muddle about metempsychosis, A said, but even Bloom's level of culture is nothing to shout about, B said, or to write home about, there are also people who find her selfish and humorless, C said, to me she almost always seems very funny, B said, so much so that she sometimes wets herself laughing, A said, perhaps referring to the time she had to rush to the women's toilet at the DBC on Dame Street, and left her suede gloves on the seat, pull the chain of Molly's incredible associations and flush away, C said, and the Cicerone had said as much when he went in, we are still in Molly's bed, in the bed of her stream of consciousness, which is overflowing, A said and will flow uncontrollably for more than half an hour, C said, from shortly after two in the morning, B pointed out, if we can speak of time in the genital infinite of the eternal female, Professor Jones argued, going on to explain that the eight o'clock of the first chapter of *Ulysses* is contained in this last one, ∞, the *double symbol* of infinity and Molly's genitals, and of course, the Professor continued, the other cardinal points in the chapter that Joyce mentioned besides the breasts are the ass—this chapter is the colophon or rear end of the book, according to Joyce, A said—Please!, yes, the ass, the belly, and the cunt, which make up the female universe, Professor Jones added, Molly's world more like, A said, she gushes on with her stream of thoughts while Poldy is sleeping like a log beside her, to serve or not serve him his breakfast in bed in the morning, C said, that is the question Molly is mulling over throughout eight long sentences without punctuation, eight long phases, Professor Jones said, like the eight big poppies Poldy the man with an eye for detail once sent her on her birthday, A said, which was the eighth of September, the Virgin's birthday, C said, and to continue with the eight debate, A said, Molly married Bloom on the eighth of October, 1888, when she was eighteen, and eight days from now she has to go to Belfast with Boylan, B said, and in a Bovarian way she thinks he will travel first class, and above all she imagines the rattling, A said, and the toing and froing with him in the tunnel of love, the toings and froings with Boylan as you say, and which Molly imagines without compunction, B said, without punctuation, said A, and among other things she tells us that Boylan went out for a moment to buy the *Evening Telegraph*, then angrily tore up his betting tickets when he discovered his horse hadn't won—he never thought of betting on

Throwaway—B said, and on the dresser Bloom has seen the proof of suitor Boylan's defeat, Molly did not like at all his manners and his roughness, *vorrei e non vorrei*, A said, she liked them and did not like them, Molly also wonders if she really pleases Boylan, and the poor woman also wonders if she gave him pleasure, said B, because he fell asleep after the last bout of love-making, and next time she will try out new positions, said A, she will tell Boylan to come into her from behind like Mrs. Mastiansky said her husband did, and the mastiffs, oh be careful with dogs, C said, because after watching how two mongrel dogs mated in the street she became *embarazada* with Rudy, then she goes over the clothes she needs, B said, above all drawers and a corset that fits like a glove, A said, she wants to keep her shape, and says she has too much belly, she ought to give up beer, B recalled, but that *embonpoint* is by no means Molly's weak point, A said, and she goes on to other erogenous zones, to the first cardinal point, Professor Jones said, and after remembering Boylan enjoying her jewels, A said, she crosses the strait and relives her first adventures in Gibraltar, for example the one-eyed Moor who sang braying with "his heass of an instrument," she evokes the first kiss in Gibraltar under the Moorish wall, and her fear of getting *embarazada*, B said, one of the first words she learned in Spanish, said A, but she consoled herself with a banana, even though she was frightened it might get stuck inside, and she also consoles her first love, Mulvey, with her hand, B said, although she no longer clearly remembers what his first name was, C said, and she unbuttoned Mulvey whatsisname, A said, took it out, slid back the foreskin and stared at the kind of eye on the end, then made it stand up and went on playing with his peaked *H.M.S. Calypso* navy cap, Professor Jones digressed, and from the cove at Gibraltar she moves to the choir stairs with Bartell d'Arcy, in an *Ave Maria*, to her ablutions after her fuck with Boylan, and in spite of the rumblings she tries not to make any noise so as not to wake Poldy, and *piano piano* she lets out *pianissimo* a furtive fart as a train whistles by, using the same ruse Poldy himself employed at the end of "Sirens," said B, she also tries not to make any noise when she pees into the chamber pot, A said, the waters of Lahore the whore, which flow into the Red Sea, at least Boylan hasn't left her pregnant as Bloom feared, B said, and after putting on a sanitary napkin she returns to bed to fantasize about Stephen, the young stranger who appeared in the cards, C said, then recalling again in the Gibraltar bed, A said, the night-boat trip from Tarifa to Europa Point, the moon and the lighthouse, the halo, the ideal beauty of naked young boys on the Gibraltar beach of Margate, the youthful and pretty prick on a statue, she wouldn't mind at all putting that in her mouth, or the prick of a young poet like Stephen, it would fill her with glory, and she contrasts this with Boylan's rough treatment, C said who when it came down to it had less spunk and a lot less brain than her Poldy, A said, that vulgar playboy Boylan, slapping her buttocks and parading his erection around, and she makes plans to teach Stephen Spanish and thinks she will take him breakfast in bed, *dos huevos estrellados senor*, although kind Poldy could serve her and Stephen breakfast too, said B, in her mind she is already thinking of their ménage à trois, C said, a trinity in which Stephen is fundamentally a young, idealized Bloom, said Professor Jones, two different people and only one true Bloom, A said, the cuckold ends up being truly

Coronado, king of the house, C said, almost imperceptibly through the idealized Stephen, Molly starts to accept Bloom or *Stoom*, A said, she will give him another chance, C said, she will get up early the next morning to go to the market and make him his breakfast, but since it's now about two in the morning, B said, I suspect that despite her good intentions, Molly will stay stuck to the sheets with her fleshy cheeks come daylight, said A, and she plans the seduction of Sinbad the Husband, snoring at her side, past fast asleep, C said, by the light of the lamp Molly sees the stars of the wallpaper they had in their Lombard Street house, B said, she will say to her husband the yes I will yes, C said, Zerlina's *yes* from *Don Giovanni*, Professor Jones said, which she has been rehearsing all day, adding, the body always affirming in a frankly affirmative novel, although it seems to me, C replied, that there are more *Nos* than *Yesses* in *Ulysses*, aren't there? And the Macintosh screen shone briefly

NO: 640   YES: 354

then switched off again when the Cicerone, who'd been keeping quiet, flashed his wand at it, the sun of the new day will shine perhaps for Molly and Bloom, C said, and she rolls again in the rhododendrons at Howth, said A, in Bloom's arms, and Bloom's kiss is the kiss of first love, Mulvey Everyman and Noman, like Ulysses, and she, the Andalusian girl with the rose in her hair, will say the definitive yes, we agree, the yes of the beginning and end, to feel her breasts, close the circle, loop the loop, as round as the earth that goes on turning, the sun of a new day is going to shine and it is the yes of *finis*, the last word, yes, yes, yes, three times, we insist, we persist, but with his blind man's stick the Cicerone pointed to the screen that had lit up once more, as though to show us that these were the real last words of *Ulysses*, those of the odyssey of its writing:

Trieste-Zurich-Paris
1914–1921

Exit

We had been through all the rooms, galleries, corridors, and passageways of the House of Ulysses, sometimes retracing our steps, take a second look the Cicerone seemed to tell us with all the patience in the world, although now he was shepherding us quickly toward the exit with his wand, back to the book, we thought we heard him say, and B followed his advice, taking two or three long strides, sitting on a lower step, showing us her tanned thighs, and beginning to read a letter or saucy postcard in such a subdued voice we only managed to hear scattered phrases: . . . and she brought me breakfast in bed, *dos huevos estrellados, señor,* and burst out laughing at me in the battered old bed that started to creak once more beneath our kiss . . . then came back to bed to dream of the silhouette of the Rock rising like a giant when the east wind blew black as night, and she felt nostalgia for the south, for another night on the tiles in Ronda, for its inns and castanets, for the first man who put his tongue in her mouth, kissing her morosely under the Moorish wall, and she said farewell to him with her handkerchief wet with tears, bursting with emotion, the day before her departure, a beautiful, blooming day in May, in the fir-tree cove, and she would wear a rose in her hair again like the Andalusian girls did, and deep in her bed sing deep-throated gypsy songs, "Anda Jaleo" . . . and repeat over and over *ad sexeam* all the obscene phrases of . . . B went on in a low voice, until high above her the Cicerone signed off with a flourish of his wand.

JULIÁN RÍOS is Spain's foremost postmodernist writer. After co-authoring two books with Octavio Paz, Ríos has gone on to write numerous works of fiction and nonfiction, including *Larva, Poundemonium, Loves That Bind*, and *Monstruary*, all of which have been published in English translation. He lives in Paris.

NICK CAISTOR is a translator, editor, and author. He has written a biography of Octavio Paz and has translated the works of José Saramago and Paulo Coelho, among others.

SELECTED DALKEY ARCHIVE PAPERBACKS

PETROS ABATZOGLOU, *What Does Mrs. Freeman Want?*
MICHAL AJVAZ, *The Golden Age.*
The Other City.
PIERRE ALBERT-BIROT, *Grabinoulor.*
YUZ ALESHKOVSKY, *Kangaroo.*
FELIPE ALFAU, *Chromos.*
Locos.
IVAN ÂNGELO, *The Celebration.*
The Tower of Glass.
DAVID ANTIN, *Talking.*
ANTÓNIO LOBO ANTUNES, *Knowledge of Hell.*
ALAIN ARIAS-MISSON, *Theatre of Incest.*
IFTIKHAR ARIF AND WAQAS KHWAJA, EDS., *Modern Poetry of Pakistan.*
JOHN ASHBERY AND JAMES SCHUYLER, *A Nest of Ninnies.*
HEIMRAD BÄCKER, *transcript.*
DJUNA BARNES, *Ladies Almanack.*
Ryder.
JOHN BARTH, *LETTERS.*
Sabbatical.
DONALD BARTHELME, *The King.*
Paradise.
SVETISLAV BASARA, *Chinese Letter.*
RENÉ BELLETTO, *Dying.*
MARK BINELLI, *Sacco and Vanzetti Must Die!*
ANDREI BITOV, *Pushkin House.*
ANDREJ BLATNIK, *You Do Understand.*
LOUIS PAUL BOON, *Chapel Road.*
My Little War.
Summer in Termuren.
ROGER BOYLAN, *Killoyle.*
IGNÁCIO DE LOYOLA BRANDÃO, *Anonymous Celebrity.*
The Good-Bye Angel.
Teeth under the Sun.
Zero.
BONNIE BREMSER, *Troia: Mexican Memoirs.*
CHRISTINE BROOKE-ROSE, *Amalgamemnon.*
BRIGID BROPHY, *In Transit.*
MEREDITH BROSNAN, *Mr. Dynamite.*
GERALD L. BRUNS, *Modern Poetry and the Idea of Language.*
EVGENY BUNIMOVICH AND J. KATES, EDS., *Contemporary Russian Poetry: An Anthology.*
GABRIELLE BURTON, *Heartbreak Hotel.*
MICHEL BUTOR, *Degrees.*
Mobile.
Portrait of the Artist as a Young Ape.
G. CABRERA INFANTE, *Infante's Inferno.*
Three Trapped Tigers.
JULIETA CAMPOS, *The Fear of Losing Eurydice.*
ANNE CARSON, *Eros the Bittersweet.*
ORLY CASTEL-BLOOM, *Dolly City.*
CAMILO JOSÉ CELA, *Christ versus Arizona.*
The Family of Pascual Duarte.
The Hive.
LOUIS-FERDINAND CÉLINE, *Castle to Castle.*
Conversations with Professor Y.
London Bridge.

Normance.
North.
Rigadoon.
HUGO CHARTERIS, *The Tide Is Right.*
JEROME CHARYN, *The Tar Baby.*
MARC CHOLODENKO, *Mordechai Schamz.*
JOSHUA COHEN, *Witz.*
EMILY HOLMES COLEMAN, *The Shutter of Snow.*
ROBERT COOVER, *A Night at the Movies.*
STANLEY CRAWFORD, *Log of the S.S. The Mrs Unguentine.*
Some Instructions to My Wife.
ROBERT CREELEY, *Collected Prose.*
RENÉ CREVEL, *Putting My Foot in It.*
RALPH CUSACK, *Cadenza.*
SUSAN DAITCH, *L.C.*
Storytown.
NICHOLAS DELBANCO, *The Count of Concord.*
NIGEL DENNIS, *Cards of Identity.*
PETER DIMOCK, *A Short Rhetoric for Leaving the Family.*
ARIEL DORFMAN, *Konfidenz.*
COLEMAN DOWELL, *The Houses of Children.*
Island People.
Too Much Flesh and Jabez.
ARKADII DRAGOMOSHCHENKO, *Dust.*
RIKKI DUCORNET, *The Complete Butcher's Tales.*
The Fountains of Neptune.
The Jade Cabinet.
The One Marvelous Thing.
Phosphor in Dreamland.
The Stain.
The Word "Desire."
WILLIAM EASTLAKE, *The Bamboo Bed.*
Castle Keep.
Lyric of the Circle Heart.
JEAN ECHENOZ, *Chopin's Move.*
STANLEY ELKIN, *A Bad Man.*
Boswell: A Modern Comedy.
Criers and Kibitzers, Kibitzers and Criers.
The Dick Gibson Show.
The Franchiser.
George Mills.
The Living End.
The MacGuffin.
The Magic Kingdom.
Mrs. Ted Bliss.
The Rabbi of Lud.
Van Gogh's Room at Arles.
ANNIE ERNAUX, *Cleaned Out.*
LAUREN FAIRBANKS, *Muzzle Thyself.*
Sister Carrie.
LESLIE A. FIEDLER, *Love and Death in the American Novel.*
JUAN FILLOY, *Op Oloop.*
GUSTAVE FLAUBERT, *Bouvard and Pécuchet.*
KASS FLEISHER, *Talking out of School.*
FORD MADOX FORD, *The March of Literature.*
JON FOSSE, *Aliss at the Fire.*
Melancholy.

FOR A FULL LIST OF PUBLICATIONS, VISIT:
www.dalkeyarchive.com

SELECTED DALKEY ARCHIVE PAPERBACKS

FOR A FULL LIST OF PUBLICATIONS, VISIT:
www.dalkeyarchive.com

My Life in CIA.
Singular Pleasures.
The Sinking of the Odradek
  Stadium.
Tlooth.
20 Lines a Day.
JOSEPH MCELROY,
  Night Soul and Other Stories.
ROBERT L. MCLAUGHLIN, ED.,
  Innovations: An Anthology of
  Modern & Contemporary Fiction.
HERMAN MELVILLE, *The Confidence-Man.*
AMANDA MICHALOPOULOU, *I'd Like.*
STEVEN MILLHAUSER,
  The Barnum Museum.
  In the Penny Arcade.
RALPH J. MILLS, JR.,
  Essays on Poetry.
MOMUS, *The Book of Jokes.*
CHRISTINE MONTALBETTI, *Western.*
OLIVE MOORE, *Spleen.*
NICHOLAS MOSLEY, *Accident.*
  Assassins.
  Catastrophe Practice.
  Children of Darkness and Light.
  Experience and Religion.
  God's Hazard.
  The Hesperides Tree.
  Hopeful Monsters.
  Imago Bird.
  Impossible Object.
  Inventing God.
  Judith.
  Look at the Dark.
  Natalie Natalia.
  Paradoxes of Peace.
  Serpent.
  Time at War.
  The Uses of Slime Mould:
  Essays of Four Decades.
WARREN MOTTE,
  Fables of the Novel: French Fiction
  since 1990.
  Fiction Now: The French Novel in
  the 21st Century.
  Oulipo: A Primer of Potential
  Literature.
YVES NAVARRE, *Our Share of Time.*
  Sweet Tooth.
DOROTHY NELSON, *In Night's City.*
  Tar and Feathers.
ESHKOL NEVO, *Homesick.*
WILFRIDO D. NOLLEDO,
  But for the Lovers.
FLANN O'BRIEN,
  At Swim-Two-Birds.
  At War.
  The Best of Myles.
  The Dalkey Archive.
  Further Cuttings.
  The Hard Life.
  The Poor Mouth.
  The Third Policeman.
CLAUDE OLLIER, *The Mise-en-Scène.*
PATRIK OUŘEDNÍK, *Europeana.*
BORIS PAHOR, *Necropolis.*

FERNANDO DEL PASO,
  News from the Empire.
  Palinuro of Mexico.
ROBERT PINGET, *The Inquisitory.*
  Mahu or The Material.
  Trio.
MANUEL PUIG,
  Betrayed by Rita Hayworth.
  The Buenos Aires Affair.
  Heartbreak Tango.
RAYMOND QUENEAU, *The Last Days.*
  Odile.
  Pierrot Mon Ami.
  Saint Glinglin.
ANN QUIN, *Berg.*
  Passages.
  Three.
  Tripticks.
ISHMAEL REED,
  The Free-Lance Pallbearers.
  The Last Days of Louisiana Red.
  Ishmael Reed: The Plays.
  Reckless Eyeballing.
  The Terrible Threes.
  The Terrible Twos.
  Yellow Back Radio Broke-Down.
JEAN RICARDOU, *Place Names.*
RAINER MARIA RILKE, *The Notebooks of*
  Malte Laurids Brigge.
JULIÁN RÍOS, *The House of Ulysses.*
  Larva: A Midsummer Night's Babel.
  Poundemonium.
AUGUSTO ROA BASTOS, *I the Supreme.*
DANIÈL ROBBERECHTS,
  Arriving in Avignon.
OLIVIER ROLIN, *Hotel Crystal.*
ALIX CLEO ROUBAUD, *Alix's Journal.*
JACQUES ROUBAUD, *The Form of a*
  City Changes Faster, Alas, Than
  the Human Heart.
  The Great Fire of London.
  Hortense in Exile.
  Hortense Is Abducted.
  The Loop.
  The Plurality of Worlds of Lewis.
  The Princess Hoppy.
  Some Thing Black.
LEON S. ROUDIEZ,
  French Fiction Revisited.
VEDRANA RUDAN, *Night.*
STIG SÆTERBAKKEN, *Siamese.*
LYDIE SALVAYRE, *The Company of Ghosts.*
  Everyday Life.
  The Lecture.
  Portrait of the Writer as a
  Domesticated Animal.
  The Power of Flies.
LUIS RAFAEL SÁNCHEZ,
  Macho Camacho's Beat.
SEVERO SARDUY, *Cobra & Maitreya.*
NATHALIE SARRAUTE,
  Do You Hear Them?
  Martereau.
  The Planetarium.
ARNO SCHMIDT, *Collected Stories.*
  Nobodaddy's Children.

FOR A FULL LIST OF PUBLICATIONS, VISIT:
www.dalkeyarchive.com

SELECTED DALKEY ARCHIVE PAPERBACKS

FOR A FULL LIST OF PUBLICATIONS, VISIT:
www.dalkeyarchive.com